SOLOMON'S
MINES

H. Rider Haggard

KING SOLOMON'S MINES

Published in this edition 1997 by Peter Haddock Ltd,
Pinfold Lane, Bridlington, East Yorkshire YO16 5BT
Reprinted 1999

© 1997 This arrangement, text and illustrations,
Children's Leisure Products Limited, David Dale House,
New Lanark, Scotland

© Original text John Kennett

Illustrated by Graham Smith (Simon Girling Associates)

ISBN 0 7105 0940 5

Printed and bound in India

Contents

To the Reader

I am sure you will have seen a film, or watched a programme on TV, that has been made from some famous book. If you enjoyed the film or programme, you may have decided to read the book.

Then what happens? You get the book and, it's more than likely, you get a shock as well! You turn ten or twenty pages, and nothing seems to *happen*. Where are all the lively people and exciting incidents? When, you say, will the author get down to telling the story? In the end you will probably throw the book aside and give it up. Now, why is that?

Well, perhaps the author was writing for adults and not for children. Perhaps the book was written a long time ago, when people had more time for reading and liked nothing better than a book that would keep them entertained for weeks.

We think differently today. That's why I've taken some of these wonderful books, and retold them for you. If you enjoy them in this shorter form, then I hope that when you are older you will go back to the original books, and enjoy all the more the wonderful stories they have to tell.

About the Author

Henry Rider Haggard was born in Norfolk in 1856. At the age of nineteen he went out to South Africa as secretary to the Governor of Natal. He returned to England in 1881 and there settled down to a successful writing career. He was knighted in 1912 and died in 1925.

The years Rider Haggard spent in South Africa provided him with exotic settings for many of his novels, including *She, Allan Quatermain* and, the most famous, *King Solomon's Mines.* This exciting story of the strange journey made by Allan Quatermain and his companions into unknown Africa has stirred the imagination of its readers over the years.

Chapter One

A Man Called Neville

The story I am going to tell is a strange one. And I think you will agree, if you see it to the end, that it has to do with some weird and terrible things, wicked and unbelievable things, fit to curdle the blood in your veins. Certainly there were times when the blood ran cold in *my* veins.

I am not a writer by trade. I am a white hunter. My name is Allan Quatermain and I live in Durban, South Africa. I am fifty-five years of age and for more than thirty years I have been trading, hunting, fighting or mining in one part of Africa or another. I have, in my time, shot sixty-five lions. The sixty-sixth got *me* and mauled me pretty badly before he was driven off. That is why I limp a bit on my left leg.

Well, it's eighteen months or so since I first met Sir Henry Curtis and Captain Good, which is the real beginning of my story. That was in 1885. I'd been elephant hunting beyond Bamangwato and had had bad luck. Everything went wrong on that trip, and to top up with I got the fever badly.

As soon as I was well enough I sold such ivory as I had and took myself down to the Cape. After a week in Cape Town, I made up my mind to go back to Durban by the *Dunkeld*, then lying in the docks waiting for the *Edinburgh Castle* to get in from England. I took my berth and went aboard, and that afternoon the passengers from England came on and we put to sea.

Among the passengers who came on board there were two

who caught my interest. One, a man of about thirty, was one of the biggest and strongest-looking men I ever saw. He had yellow hair and beard, clear-cut features and large grey eyes set deep in his head. I found out, by looking at the passenger list, that this was Sir Henry Curtis. He reminded me very much of somebody else, but at the time I could not remember who it was.

The man with him was listed as Captain John Good, and I put him down at once as a naval officer. He was stout and dark, and very neat and very clean-shaved, and he always wore an eyeglass in his right eye.

That evening I went into the ship's lounge for a drink and a chat, and found Sir Henry and his friend already there. Somehow we got into talk about shooting elephants and a man who knew me, and who was sitting nearby, called out: "Hunter Quatermain should be able to tell you about elephants if anybody can."

Sir Henry gave a start and stared at me: "Excuse me, sir," he said, "but is your name Allan Quatermain?"

I said it was. Sir Henry and Captain Good looked at each other, then Curtis turned back to me.

"We have come from England to find you," he said. "I wish to talk with you, privately. Will you come to my cabin so that we can speak without being overheard?"

I was puzzled, but said I would. The cabin was a very good one. Sir Henry poured drinks and then said: "Mr. Quatermain, the year before last about this time you were, I believe, at a place called Bamangwato, to the north of the Transvaal?"

"Yes," I answered, surprised that he should know it.

"Did you happen to meet a man called Neville there?"

"Neville? Why, yes—he camped alongside of me for a week or

two. I had a letter from a lawyer a few months back asking if I knew what had become of him."

"I know," Curtis said. "Your reply was sent on to me. It was not very *clear*, Mr. Quatermain. Tell me, do you know where Mr.—er—Mr. Neville was going?"

"I did hear something," I said, and stopped there.

Then came a pause. Curtis and Good looked at each other, and finally Good nodded his head. Sir Henry turned back to me.

"I'm going to tell you the truth," he said. "The man you knew as Neville was my brother."

I sat up and slapped my leg. "Of course! I see it now there's a real likeness."

"Yes," Curtis said. "Five years ago, just before my father died, I quarrelled with my brother George. My father had put off making his will until it was too late and, as the eldest son, I inherited all his property. My brother was naturally bitter about this. I intended to make up the quarrel with him and share the inheritance, but before I could do so he took the name of Neville and set off for Africa, in the hope of making a fortune, I suppose. That was three years ago and I've heard nothing from him since. I'm deeply troubled about him and I've come out here to find him."

"Perhaps, sir," said the captain, "you'll tell us what you know about Mr. Neville?"

Sir Henry leaned forward and stared straight into my eyes. "What was it you heard at Bamangwato, about my brother's journey?"

"I heard that he was looking for Solomon's Mines."

I gazed from one to the other. Both were staring at me.

"Solomon's Mines!" they exclaimed together. "Where are they?"

"I know where they are said to be," I answered. "Beyond some mountains that I once saw . . . the Suliman Berg or Solomon's Mountains, they're called—but there were a hundred and thirty miles of desert between me and them. There's a legend in Africa that it was somewhere up to the north of the Suliman Berg that King Solomon had his diamond mines."

Curtis was frowning at me, eyebrows tight drawn.

"Good Lord!" he said. "King Solomon of the Bible? It can't be true!"

"Why not?" I asked. "I've been a long time in Africa, gentlemen, and I've seen some odd things and heard some odd tales. But none more curious than the one I'm going to tell you now."

I got to my feet and began to pace the cabin floor, wondering how I should tell it, while they watched me and waited for my tale. And as I paced, the memories came flooding back and I saw again in my mind's eye the face of a dying man and heard him gasp out his last words beside my camp fire all those years ago....

Chapter Two

The Legend of Solomon's Mines

"It must be ten years," I said, "since I first heard the legend of Solomon's Mines. I was up-country at a place called Sitanda's Kraal, a God-forsaken spot on the edge of the desert, when a

Portuguese arrived. He was tall and thin, with large grey moustaches, and he told me his name was José Silvestre.

When he went on next day he said: 'Goodbye, senhor. If ever we meet again, I shall be the richest man in the world!'

I laughed and watched him strike out across the great desert to the west, wondering if he was mad, or what he thought he was going to find there. A week passed, and one evening I was sitting by my fire when suddenly out there in the desert I heard someone calling: 'Water! For the love of God, water!'

It was the voice of José Silvestre. And then, in the moonlight, I saw him—or I saw a figure—on a slope of rising ground only a hundred feet away. It was creeping on hands and knees, then it got up and staggered a few yards, only to fall and crawl again.

I ran towards him. He was on his hands and knees when I reached him. I helped him up and he felt no heavier than his skeleton and a bit of skin. It was José Silvestre, all right. In the moon's light, he looked ghastly. His large, dark eyes stood nearly out of his head, for all his flesh had gone. I lifted him in my arms and he seemed to weigh nothing at all. I laid him on a blanket by my camp fire, then fetched my water bottle. Propping him against my knee, I gave him water, making him take a little at a time. All at once he pushed the bottle from him and began to rave.

'The mountains!' he gasped out. 'Must get over the mountains—find diamonds—the bright stones. But—ah, no!—the desert—burning—burning—'

'Easy, Silvestre,' I said. 'You're safe now.'

He quietened down and drank again from my bottle. I fed him a little biscuit soaked in water, then laid him back and he went to sleep. My own bed I made close by. I slept on and off and

several times during the night he wakened and mumbled and I gave him water.

At dawn I woke again, and in the half light saw him sitting up, a strange gaunt form, gazing out across the desert. The first ray of the sun shot right across the wide plain before us till it reached the far-away crest of one of the tallest of the Suliman Mountains more than a hundred miles away.

'There it is!' cried the dying man, 'but I shall never reach it, never. No one will ever reach it!'

Suddenly he paused and seemed to make up his mind. 'Friend,' he said, 'are you there? My eyes grow dark.'

I wriggled out of my blankets and went to him. 'Yes,' I said, 'yes, lie down now and rest.'

'I shall rest soon enough,' he said. 'Listen. I am dying. You have been good to me. I will give you the paper. Perhaps you will get there if you can live through the desert. Be quick, friend— the paper—inside my shirt. Here, take it.'

He groped inside his shirt and brought out a pouch made of antelope skin and fastened with a little strip of hide. This he tried to untie, but could not.

'Untie it,' he said.

I did so and took out a bit of torn yellow linen, on which something was written in rusty letters. Inside was a paper.

'My friend,' Silvestre said weakly, 'I give to you the writing and the map made by my ancestor, José da Silvestra, three hundred years ago, when he was dying on Solomon's Mountains. His slave brought it home to Delagoa. Ah, it has been the death of me, that writing. I did not find the diamonds, but you may succeed and become the richest man in the world! Only give it to no one. Go yourself.'

'I'll go,' I told him. 'Do not tire yourself any more.'

'Yes,' he breathed. 'I will rest now. I will rest—'

His head fell back and he was still. I felt his heart and pulse, but I knew that he was dead. We buried him deep, that morning, with big boulders on his chest, so I do not think that the jackals can have dug him up. Then we struck camp and left Sitanda's Kraal."

There had been a picture in my mind, but now it faded. A voice was speaking to me, impatiently. I came to with a start, and was back in the first-class cabin on the *Dunkeld* and two men were regarding me strangely.

"The document," Sir Henry was saying. "The scrap of linen and the paper? Come, man, tell us more."

"Very well," I said, and took out my pocket book. I opened it. "I have here a copy of each. I've not shown them to anyone else, except to an old Portuguese trader, who translated the writing for me. He was drunk at the time, and had forgotten all about it the next morning. The original rag is at my home in Durban. Here is a copy of the map, if it can be called that."

They bent over it eagerly.

"It's all there," said Good excitedly; "the desert, Solomon's Mountains—and look—mouth of treasure cave!"

"What was written on the linen?" asked Sir Henry.

"This," I said, and began to read:

I, José da Silvestra, who am now dying of hunger in the little cave where no snow is on the north side of the nipple of the southernmost of the two mountains I have named Sheba's Breasts, write this in the year 1590 with a cleft bone upon a remnant of my raiment, my blood being the ink. If my slave

should find it when he comes, and should bring it to Delagoa, let my friend (name illegible) bring the matter to the knowledge of the king, that he may send an army which, if they live through the desert and the mountains, and can overcome the brave Kukuanas and their devilish arts, to which end many priests should be brought, will make him the richest king since Solomon. With my own eyes have I seen the countless diamonds stored in Solomon's treasure chamber behind the White Death; but through the treachery of Gagool the witchfinder I might bring nought away, scarcely my life. Let him who comes follow the map, and climb the snow of Sheba's left breast till he comes to the nipple, on the north side of which is the great road Solomon made, from whence three days' journey to the King's Palace. Let him kill Gagool. Pray for my soul. Farewell.

José da Silvestra

There was a little silence and then: "Well," said Captain Good, "I'm hanged if I ever heard a yarn like that out of a story book, or in it either, for that matter!"

"It's an odd tale, Mr. Quatermain," said Sir Henry thoughtfully.

"Yes, Sir Henry, and your brother went off into the desert with the idea of crossing Solomon's Mountains and finding the diamonds."

"So that's what he was after?"

"I don't know how he got hold of the story," I said. "He told me he'd got to make his fortune somehow, so he might as well have a fling for the diamonds. He wouldn't be talked out of it. He started across the desert with one bearer, a Kafir hunter called Jim, and, well gentlemen, I'm very much afraid—"

"Mr. Quatermain," said Sir Henry, "I'm going to look for my brother. I'm going to Solomon's Mountains, and over them if need be, and I'll keep looking until I find him or know that he is dead. Will you come with me?"

"No, Sir Henry," I said firmly. "I'm sorry, but I'm too old for wild-goose chases of that sort."

"Oh, come, sir," said Captain Good, "We need you. You know the country and the people."

"I'm a rich man," Sir Henry went on. "I'll pay you whatever you ask within reason. I'm willing to pay all expenses, and any diamonds that we find will belong to you and Good equally. I do not want them."

"Didn't you promise that Portuguese chappie you'd have a shot at finding his diamonds?" asked Good.

"Yes," I said thoughtfully, "I did." I came to a decision. "All right, gentlemen, I'll go."

"Good man!" said Curtis.

"If you'll pay me five hundred pounds for the trip—"

"It's settled," said Curtis eagerly.

"Then I undertake to serve you to the best of my ability."

Curtis held out his hand, saying "I am immensely grateful to you. Let's drink on it."

"I doubt if we'll persuade a single native to come one step further than Sitanda's Kraal," I told him as he poured the whisky. "The natives are terrified of the desert."

He handed me my glass and I raised it. "I'll give you a toast. The other side of the desert! May we reach there without harm!"

"The other side of the desert!" cried Curtis and Good, and I drank my whisky. Then I said goodnight and turned in, and dreamt about poor long-dead José da Silvestra and the diamonds.

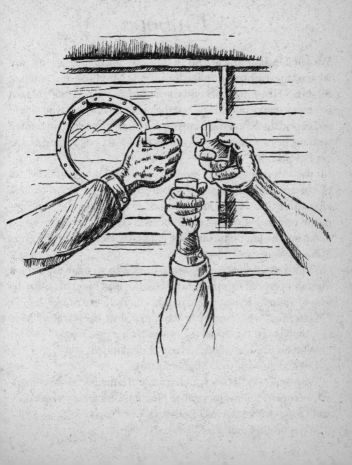

Chapter Three

Umbopa

We left Durban at the end of January and, after a long and wearisome tramp of many hundreds of miles, we reached Sitanda's Kraal in the second week of May. We had half a dozen bearers to carry our things, but the only one of them who would go beyond the Kraal was Ventvögel, a Hottentot who had hunted with me before and who was one of the most perfect game trackers I ever knew.

It was evening when we pitched camp, and the great fiery ball of the sun was sinking into the desert. Leaving Good to look after things, Sir Henry and I walked to the top of the slope opposite and gazed out across the desert. Far, far away we could make out the faint blue outlines, capped with white, of the great Suliman Berg.

We looked in silence and, as we turned to go back to camp, a man stepped out from behind a boulder and lifted his spear by way of salute. He was a tall, handsome Zulu warrior.

"Greetings, white men," he said, in a slow, deep voice. "Men say that you go far across the desert. Is it a true word?"

"Why do you ask where we go?" I demanded.

"I would go with you, Macumazahn."

("Macumazahn" is my Kafir name and it means "he who keeps his eyes open"; Curtis they called "Incubu", meaning "elephant", and Good was known as "Bougwan", or "glass eye".)

"What do they call you?" I asked.

"Umbopa."

"Where is your kraal?"

"I have no kraal," he answered simply. "I have wandered for many years. The house of my tribe is in the far north and now I would return to them. I want no money, but I am a brave man and worth my meat."

"What does he say, Quatermain?" Sir Henry asked, studying Umbopa with keen eyes.

"He wants to come with us, and without pay, too. I don't like it. Somehow, he is very different from the ordinary run of Zulus."

"He's a fine-looking man," Sir Henry said. "Strong as an ox, I'll be bound."

"Umbopa," I said, "take off your coat."

He slipped off his coat and stood before us, naked except for his loincloth and a necklace of lions' claws. I never saw a finer looking African. Standing about six foot three, he was broad as well as shapely, but light-coloured for a Zulu, and it puzzled me.

Sir Henry walked up to him and looked into his proud, handsome face. They made a good pair; both the same height and build, one as big as the other. Curtis turned back to me.

"I like his looks," he said. "I'll take him as my servant."

"The white lord will take you as his servant," I told Umbopa in Zulu.

"It is good," Umbopa said, and looked Sir Henry in the eye. "We are men, you and I."

He turned to me. "Be my mouth, Macumazahn, and say my words to my master, for I would speak to him."

"Well, this is an impudent rogue!" I said with a half laugh. "He asks me to translate, for he would speak to you."

"All right, let's hear what he has to say."

"Speak then, Umbopa," I said in Zulu.

"The desert is wide and there is no water in it," he said. "The mountains are high and covered with snow. How shall you come to the other side, and why do you go, my master?"

"The white lord goes because a man of his blood, his brother, has gone there before him. He journeys to find him."

Umbopa gave a laugh. "It seems that we are much alike, the white lord and I. Perhaps I, too, seek a brother over the mountains."

I looked at him suspiciously. "What do you know of those mountains?" I asked.

"A little, a very little," he answered mysteriously. "There is a strange land, yonder: it is a land of witchcraft and evil, and also a land of very many beautiful things; a land of brave people, of snowy peaks, and of a great white road. I have heard of it, white man."

Again I looked at him doubtfully. The man knew too much. He read my look.

"You need not fear me, white man," he said. "I dig no holes for you to fall in."

"He talks of a strange land on the other side of the mountains," I told Sir Henry.

"What does he know of it?"

"He won't say."

"I like the look of him," Curtis said. "We may be glad to have him before we're through."

"If you are to come with us," I told Umbopa, "you must come at once."

"I will come," he answered. "I have no woman to weep at my

going. I will go with you across the desert and over the mountains."

Without another word he lifted his spear in salute and strode off towards the camp.

Chapter Four

Water! Water!

Next day we made ready to start. We dismissed our bearers and arranged the kit we five—Sir Henry, Good, myself, Umbopa, and the Hottentot, Ventvögel—were to take with us. By the promise of a good hunting knife each, I managed to persuade three natives from the village to come with us for the first twenty miles, to carry each a large gourd holding a gallon of water. This would mean that we could refill our water bottles after the first night's march, for we planned to start in the cool of the night.

All next day we rested and slept, and at sunset ate a hearty meal of fresh beef washed down with tea. The moon rose about nine. We made ready and moved out on to the slope at the desert's edge. We three white men stood there by ourselves. Umbopa, spear in hand and a rifle across his shoulders, a few paces ahead of us, looked out fixedly across the desert; the three hired natives, with the gourds of water, and Ventvögel, were gathered in a little knot behind.

"And now," said Sir Henry, "*trek.*"

So we started on about as strange a journey as men can make in this world, tramping through the night and in the heavy sand.

I will not weary you by telling of every step we made during the next few days. Let it be enough to say that our hired natives turned back the next afternoon. They had had enough of the desert and no number of knives would have tempted them to come a step farther. So we had a hearty drink, filled up our water bottles, and started on.

By day we rested in the shade of boulders, or dug holes in the sand, into which we crept, then pulled bushes over the hole to shield us from the sun. The heat was appalling. We always woke up feeling that we were being baked through and through.

When the moon rose, we trudged wearily on through the night, till the burning sun put an end to our labours once more.

By the end of the third night we had covered some fifty miles of desert. The map drawn by old da Silvestra marks the desert as being forty leagues across; the "pan bad water" is set down in the middle of it. Now forty leagues is one hundred and twenty miles, so by this time we should have been within twelve or fifteen miles of the water if any were there. It had better be, I thought grimly, for we had very little left.

We marched at sunset on the fourth day and stopped at two in the morning, utterly done in, and fell asleep at the foot of a strange little hill, or sand *koppie*, about a hundred feet high.

When I awoke at dawn the air was thick with a hot murkiness I cannot describe. I sat up, rubbing my dirty face with my hands to get my gummed-up lips and eyelids apart. As the daylight grew, the others began to stir and waken too.

As soon as we were all well awake, we fell to discussing the situation, which was serious enough.

"If we do not find water we shall die," Sir Henry said.

"If we can trust to the map there should be some about," I

said, but nobody seemed to get much satisfaction from that remark.

We sat blankly staring at each other. I saw Ventvögel rise and begin to walk around the foot of the sand koppie with his eyes on the ground. Presently he stopped short, and made a throaty sound, pointing at the sand.

"What is it?" we exclaimed, and rose and went to where he was standing. I saw the tracks of some animals.

"Well," I said, "it is pretty fresh springbok spoor—what of it?"

"Springboks do not go far from water," he answered.

"No," I answered, "I forgot; and thank God for it!"

I told the others what he had said. This little discovery put new life in us. Ventvögel lifted his snub nose and sniffed the hot air. Presently he spoke again.

"I *smell* water," he said.

Just at that moment the rising sun showed so grand a sight to our astonished eyes that for a moment or two we even forgot our thirst.

There, not more than forty or fifty miles from us, glittering like silver in the rays of the morning sun, and stretching away for hundreds of miles on either side, was the great Suliman Berg. Straight before us were two enormous mountains, each at least fifteen thousand feet high, standing about a dozen miles apart, joined by a precipitous cliff or rock, and towering up in awful white solemnity straight into the sky. And on the top of each was a vast round hillock covered with snow.

"Sheba's Breasts," I breathed.

And then strange mists and clouds gathered around them and veiled them from our sight.

We remembered our thirst. It was all very well for Ventvögel

to say he could smell water but we could see no signs of it. There was nothing but arid sweltering sand and karoo scrub. We walked round the hillock; there was no sign of a pan, a pool, or a spring.

"You are a fool," I said angrily to Ventvögel. "There is no water."

But still he lifted his ugly snub nose and sniffed.

"I smell it, Baas," he answered. "It is somewhere in the air."

"Yes," I said, "no doubt it is in the clouds, and about two months from now it will fall and wash our bones."

Sir Henry stroked his beard thoughtfully. "Perhaps it is on top of the hill," he suggested.

"Rot," said Good. "Whoever heard of water being found on the top of a hill?"

"Let us go and look," I put in, and without any real hope we scrambled up the sandy side of the hill, Umbopa leading. Presently he stopped as though he was petrified.

"Here is water!" he cried in a loud voice.

Chapter Five

The Cave

We rushed up to Umbopa. There, sure enough, in a deep cup on top of the sand koppie was a pool of blackish water. In another second we were all down on our stomachs drinking our fill. When we had done that we tore off our clothes and sat down in it, taking in the moisture through our parched skins.

All that day we rested, setting off again when the moon rose, having filled both ourselves and our bottles. We made good

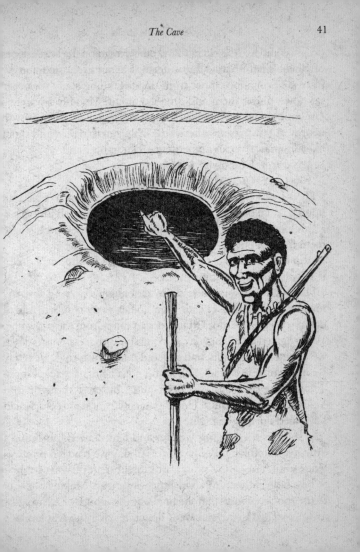

progress and two days later found ourselves upon the lower slopes
of Sheba's left breast. Our water was again exhausted and we
were suffering once more from thirst. Finding some rocks, we
sat down under them and groaned aloud. Moodily I watched
Umbopa get up and hobble off towards a patch of green growth
nearby. A few minutes afterwards he began to dance and shout
like a maniac, waving something green in his hand.

"What is it, Umbopa?" I shouted.

"Food and water, Macumazahn!" he shouted.

Then I saw what he had found. It was a melon. We had come
upon a patch of wild melons, thousands of them, all just ripe.

"Melons!" I yelled to Good, and in seconds he had his false
teeth fixed in one.

I think we ate about six each before we had done and I doubt
if I ever thought anything nicer.

That night we went on again by moonlight, carrying as many
melons as we could. The air grew cooler as we climbed, and at
dawn we were not more than a dozen miles from the snow line.
We struggled on all that day, making slow progress. At sundown
we halted for the night, and suffered much from cold. Next day
we made only five miles, and found nothing to eat except snow.
That night the cold was even more bitter. I thought that
Ventvögel, who, like most Hottentots, could not stand cold, would
have died during the night.

As soon as the sun was well up and had thawed our limbs a
little, we stumbled on once more. All day we trudged on in silence until, just before sunset, we caught sight of what seemed
to be a hole in the snow, some little way ahead. Making our way
to the spot, we found that the hole was the mouth of a cave. Just
as we reached it the sun went down, leaving the whole place

nearly dark. We crept inside and, huddling together for warmth tried to forget our miseries in sleep.

Not long before dawn I heard Ventvögel, whose teeth had been chattering all night, give a deep sigh, and then his teeth stopped chattering. His back was resting against mine, and it seemed to grow colder and colder, till at last it was like ice.

At length the air grew grey with light and the sun looked in upon our half-frozen forms—and upon Ventvögel, sitting there amongst us stone dead. No wonder his back had felt cold, poor fellow. Shocked beyond measure we dragged ourselves from the corpse and left it sitting there with its arms clasped round its knees.

By this time the sunlight was pouring its cold rays in at the mouth of the cave. Suddenly hearing an exclamation of fear from someone I turned my head to look into the cave. This was what I saw: sitting at the end of the cave was another form, of which the head rested on the chest and the long arms hung down. It too was a *dead man*, and, what was more, a white man.

The others saw it as well and the sight proved too much for our shattered nerves. One and all we scrambled out of the cave as fast as our half-frozen limbs would allow.

Chapter Six

Solomon's Road

Outside the cave we halted, feeling rather foolish.

"I'm going back," said Sir Henry. "It—what we saw—might be my brother."

This was a new idea and we re-entered the cave to put it to the proof. We waited till our eyes grew used to the gloom and then went up to the dead form. Sir Henry knelt and peered into its face. He gave a sigh of relief.

"Thank God, it is not my brother," he said.

Then I knelt and looked. The corpse was that of a tall man in middle life with hawk-like features, grizzled hair, and a long black moustache. The skin was yellow and stretched tightly over the bones. The body was clothed in the remains of a pair of woollen hose. Round the neck hung an ivory crucifix on a chain.

"Who on earth—?" I began.

"The old Dom, José da Silvestra, of course," said Good. "Who else?"

"Impossible," I gasped. "He died three hundred years ago."

"And what is there to stop his lasting three thousand years in this atmosphere?" asked Good. "This is where his slave left him. He could not have buried him alone. Look here," he went on, stooping down and picking up a strangely-shaped bone scraped at the end into a sharp point, "here is the 'cleft bone' that he used to draw the map."

We gazed at it astonished. There could be no doubt about it. There he sat, the dead man whose directions, written some three hundred years before, had led us to this spot. There in Good's hand was the pen with which the dead man had written them, and there round his neck was the crucifix his dying lips had kissed.

"Let us go," said Sir Henry in a low voice. "Stay, we will give him a companion," and lifting up the body of Ventvögel, he placed it near that of the old Dom. Then he stooped and with a jerk broke the rotten string of the crucifix, for his own fingers

were too cold to unfasten it. I believe he still has it. I took the pen, and it is before me as I write. Sometimes I sign my name with it.

We left those two grim occupants of the cave and, creeping out into the welcome sunshine, went on our way. When we had gone half a mile we came to the edge of the plateau. What lay below us we could not see, for the landscape was wreathed in morning mist. Presently, however, the higher layers of mist cleared a little and showed, some five hundred yards beneath us, at the end of a long slope of snow, a patch of green grass, through which a stream was running. Nor was this all. By the stream was a group of large antelopes.

Here was food in plenty if only we could get it. The beasts were fully six hundred yards off, a very long shot, but if we tried to get closer to them we should be certain to be seen against the blinding background of snow.

"We must have a try from here," said Sir Henry.

The three of us took careful aim with our express rifles, and succeeded in bringing down one of the beasts. Being unable to make a fire to cook the meat, we ate it raw, having first cooled it in the icy water of a stream. In a quarter of an hour we were changed men—our strength had come back to us.

"Thank God!" said Sir Henry, "that brute has saved our lives."

We set Umbopa to cut off as much of the best meat as we could carry, then began to inspect our surroundings. The mist had cleared so we were able to take in all the country before us.

Some five thousand feet beneath where we stood lay mile upon mile of the most lovely country. Here were dense patches of lofty forest, there a great river wound its silvery way. To the left stretched a rich, grassy plain on which we could just make out

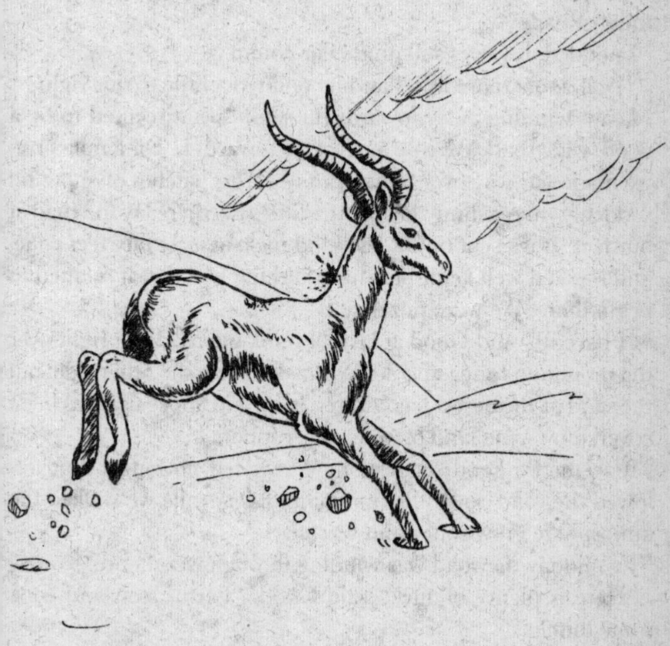

countless herds of game or cattle. To the right were more mountains with stretches of cultivated land between, amongst which we could see groups of dome-shaped huts.

We sat down for a while and gazed in silence. Presently Sir Henry spoke. "Isn't there something on the map about Solomon's Road?"

I nodded, my eyes still on the far country.

"Well, look; there it is!" and he pointed a little to our right.

I saw, winding away towards the plain, what seemed to be a good, wide road. We rose and set off towards it. For a mile or so we made our way over boulders and across patches of snow, till suddenly, on reaching the top of a little rise, there lay the road at our feet. It was cut out of the solid rock, at least fifty feet wide, and seemed well kept; but the odd thing was that it seemed to begin there. We were puzzled.

"I have it!" said Good at last. "I think the road ran right over the mountain range and across the desert on the other side, but the sand of the desert has covered it up, and above us it has been covered by some kind of volcanic eruption."

It seemed a good suggestion. We waited no longer, but followed the road down the mountain. Every mile we walked the atmosphere grew softer and warmer.

By midday the road was winding through woodland.

"Here is plenty of fuel," said Good. "Let us stop and cook some dinner."

We left the road and made our way to a stream which was babbling away not far off, and soon had a good fire of dry boughs blazing. Cutting off some hunks from the antelope meat we had brought with us, we toasted them on the end of sharp sticks and ate them with relish.

I felt drowsy then and lay back on a bed of fern, listening to Umbopa and Sir Henry trying to talk in a mixture of broken English and kitchen Zulu. Presently I missed Good and looked around for him. I spotted him by the bank of the stream, in which he had been bathing. He had on nothing but his flannel shirt. I watched him shake out his trousers, coat, and waistcoat, and fold them up neatly till he was ready to put them on, shaking his head sadly over the rips and tears in them. Then he took his boots, scrubbed them with a handful of fern, and finally rubbed them over with a piece of fat which he had saved from the meat before putting them on. Next, from a little bag he carried, he took out a pocket comb in which was fixed a tiny looking glass. He looked at himself in this and felt his chin, on which he had the scrub of a ten days' beard.

"Surely," I thought, "he is not going to try and shave."

But so it was. Taking the piece of fat with which he had greased his boots he washed it carefully in the stream. Then diving again into the bag he brought out a little safety razor, scrubbed his face and chin with the fat, and began. It was not an easy shave and he groaned very much over it. I shook with inward laughter as I watched him struggling with that stubbly beard. He had just about got the worst of it off the right side of his face and chin when I became aware of a flash of light that passed just by his head.

Good sprang up with an oath. I too got to my feet and this was what I saw: standing not twenty paces from us, and ten from Good, was a group of men, all carrying spears.

Chapter Seven
Sons of the Stars

The men were very tall and copper-coloured. Some wore plumes of feathers and short leopard-skin cloaks. In front of them stood a youth of about seventeen, his hand raised and his body bent forward in a throwing attitude. The flash of light had been a spear, and he had thrown it.

An old, soldierly-looking man stepped forward, caught the youth by the arm, and said something to him. Then they came towards us.

Sir Henry, Good and Umbopa had by this time seized their rifles and lifted them threateningly. The party of natives still came on. It struck me that they did not know what rifles were.

"Put down your guns!" I called to the others. They obeyed, and walking to the front I spoke to the elderly man.

"Greeting," I said in Zulu, not knowing what language to use. To my surprise I was understood.

"Greeting," answered the man, not, indeed, in the same tongue, but in a dialect very close to it.

"Who are you?" he went on.

"Why is it three of you have white faces, and the face of the fourth is as the face of our mother's sons?" and he pointed to Umbopa.

It flashed across me that he was right: Umbopa *was* like the men before me. I had little time to think about it, however.

"We are strangers and come in peace," I answered, "and this man is our servant."

"If you are strangers then you must die," he said. "No strangers may enter the land of the Kukuanas. It is the King's law."

I was staggered at this. The men lifted their spears.

"What did he say?" asked Good.

"He says we are going to be killed," I answered grimly.

"Oh, Lord!" groaned Good. As was his way when troubled, he put his hand to his false teeth, dragging the top set down and allowing them to fly back to his jaw with a snap. It was a lucky move, for next second the crowd of Kukuanas gave a yell of horror and bolted back some yards.

"It's his teeth," whispered Sir Henry excitedly. "He moved them. Take them out, Good, take them out!"

He obeyed, slipping the set into the sleeve of his shirt.

Soon curiosity had overcome fear, and the men advanced slowly.

"How is it, O strangers," asked the old man, "that this man" (pointing to Good, who had nothing on but his shirt, and had only half finished his shaving) "whose body is clothed, and whose legs are bare, who grows hair on one side of his sickly face and not on the other, and who has one shining and transparent eye, has teeth that move of themselves, coming away from the jaws and returning of their own will?"

"Open your mouth," I said to Good, who promptly curled up his lips and grinned at the old gentleman like an angry dog, showing to his astonished gaze two thin red lines of gum as utterly bare of teeth as a newborn elephant. The Kukuanas groaned and gasped in horror.

"Where are his teeth?" they shouted.

Good turned his head slowly and swept his hand across his mouth. Then he grinned again, and lo, there were two rows of lovely teeth.

The young man who had flung the spear threw himself down
on the grass and gave a howl of terror; and as for the old gentle
man his knees knocked together with fear.

"I see that you are spirits," he said falteringly. "Did ever man
born of woman have hair on one side of his face and not the
other, or a round and transparent eye, or teeth which move and
melt away and grow again? Pardon us, O my lords."

Here was luck indeed, and, I jumped at the chance.

"You shall be forgiven, since you knew not of our powers,"
said grandly. "Now you shall learn the truth. We come," and
pointed to the sky, "from the biggest star that shines at night."

"Oh! o-oh!" groaned the chorus of Kukuanas.

"We come to stay with you a little while, and bless you by our
visit. As you hear, I have made ready for our coming by learn
ing your language."

"It is so, it is so," put in the chorus.

"Only, my lord," said the old gentleman, "you have learned i
very badly."

I frowned at him and he backed off a little.

"I did so in haste," I told him coldly. "Now, friends, it is in my
heart to strike dead the boy who would have killed us."

I pointed to the youth, who gave a howl of terror.

"Spare him, my lords," said the old man anxiously. "He is the
king's son, and I am his uncle. If he should come to harm,
must answer for it with my own blood."

"Yes, that is so," put in the youth.

"So be it," I said. "But there may be some among you who
doubt our power to avenge. Stay, I will show you." I turned to
Umbopa and tipped a wink towards my express rifle. "Here
you dog and slave, give me the magic tube that speaks."

Umbopa handed me the rifle, making a deep bow as he did so "It is here, O lord of lords," he said.

Now, just before asking for the rifle, I had spotted a little *klipspringer* antelope standing on a mass of rock about seventy yards away, and made up my mind to risk a shot at it. I pointed it out.

"Look there," I said, "a hundred paces. What do you see?"

"Why, my lord, it is a buck," said the old man. "Shall my warriors stalk it for you?"

"There is no need," I answered. "Tell me is it possible for man born of woman to kill it from here with a noise?"

The warriors laughed heartily and jabbered among themselves.

"It is not possible, my lord," answered the old man.

"Yet shall I kill it," I said quietly.

The old man smiled, saying, "That my lord cannot do."

I raised the rifle and covered the buck. It was a small animal, but I knew that it would not do to miss.

I drew a deep breath and slowly squeezed the trigger. The buck stood still as a stone.

Bang! Thud! The buck sprang into the air and fell on the rock dead as a doornail. A groan of terror burst from the group before us.

"If you want meat," I remarked coolly, "go fetch that buck."

The old man made a sign, and one of his followers departed, and presently returned bearing the antelope. I had hit it fairly behind the shoulder. They gathered round the poor creature's body, gazing at the bullet hole in wonder.

"You see," I told them, "I do not speak empty words. If you yet doubt our power, let one of you go stand upon that rock and I will make him even as this buck."

There was a general throwing up of hands and backing away.

"Let not good magic be wasted on our poor bodies," said one warrior.

"All the witchcraft of our people cannot show the like of this," stated a second.

"It is so," agreed the old gentleman. "Listen, children of the stars; I am Infadoos, son of Kafa, once King of the Kukuana people. This youth is Scragga."

"He nearly scragged me," murmured Good.

"Scragga, son of Twala, the great king—Twala, husband of a thousand wives, lord of the Kukuanas, keeper of the great road, terror of his enemies, student of the Black Arts, leader of a hundred thousand warriors, Twala, the One-eyed, the Black, the Terrible."

"Take us then to Twala," I said in a lordly way. "We do not deal with low people and underlings."

"Yes, my lord, I will lead you to Twala and he shall see how powerful is your magic. But the way is long. We are hunting three days' journey from the place of the king."

"We are ready," I said; "lead on. But beware, Infadoos, and you, Scragga, beware! Play no monkey-tricks upon us, or the magic tubes shall talk with you loudly, and make you full of holes!"

The old man made a deep bow: "*Koom, koom,*" he said. "Let my lords have patience and we will lead them."

He turned and spoke to his warriors. They at once began picking up all our goods and chattels, in order to carry them for us; all but the guns, which they would not touch. They even seized Good's clothes, which were neatly folded up beside him. He at once made a dive for them and a loud argument followed.

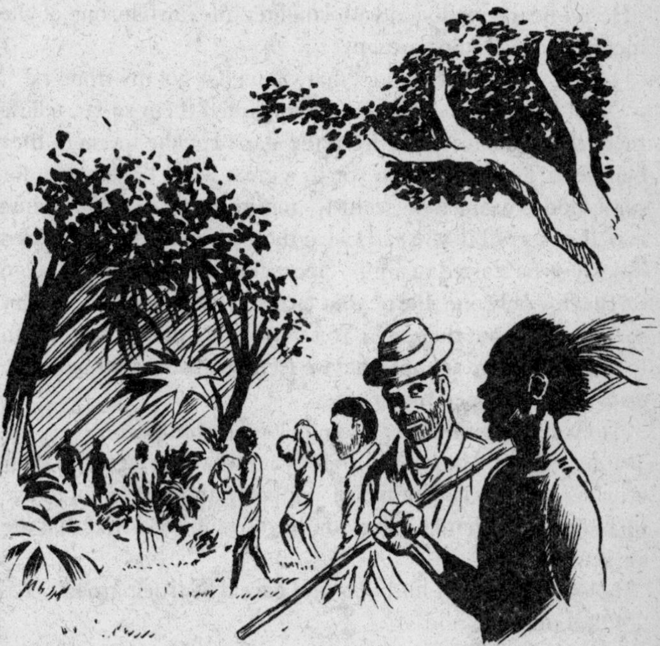

"Give me my clothes!" he cried. "I want to put them on!"

Umbopa translated.

"Let not my lord of the shining eye touch these things," Infadoos said. "Surely, his slaves shall carry them. Would my lord cover up his beautiful white legs from the eyes of his servants?"

Here I nearly exploded with laughter; meanwhile, one of the men set off with the garments.

"Damn it!" roared Good, "that villain has got my trousers!"

"Now, listen, Good," I said, "I've bluffed them so far, telling them that we have come from the stars. For the moment they believe it. They look upon you as a great witch doctor and, for some odd reason, they seem to admire your 'beautiful white legs'. I'm sorry, but you can't wear those trousers. And," I added quickly as he started to argue, "more than that, you've got to go on shaving only one side of your face and not the other. I'm very sorry for you, but there it is. You must do it, man. If they begin to suspect that we are not what we seem our lives won't be worth *that!*" and I snapped my fingers.

"Do you really think so?" asked Good gloomily.

"I do, indeed. Your teeth, your beautiful white legs, and your eyeglass are now *the* features of our party and you've got to live up to them. Be thankful that you've got your boots and that the air is warm."

He looked down at his boots and gave a heartfelt groan.

"Oh, Lord!" he said.

And then, holding his shirt-tails close to his bare legs, he began to trot after his fast disappearing trousers.

Chapter Eight

Twala the King

All that afternoon we travelled on along the great roadway, which headed in a north-westerly direction. Infadoos walked with us and I asked him who had made the road.

"None know, my lord," he answered, "not even the wise woman Gagool, the smeller out of witches, who has lived for genera-tions."

"When did the Kukuana people come into this country?"

"My lord, the race came down here ten thousand moons ago from the great lands which lie there beyond," and he pointed to the north. "They could travel no farther because of the great mountains which ring in the land. The country was good, so they settled here and grew strong and powerful. Now, when Twala the king calls up his regiments, their plumes cover the plain as far as the eye of man can reach."

"And have your soldiers fought in many wars?" I asked.

"My lord, there was one war, but it was a civil war."

"How was that?"

"My lord, Kafa the king had three sons; Imotu and Twala were born at the same birth and of the same woman. It is not our custom, lord, to suffer twins to live—the weaker must al-ways die. But the mother hid away the feebler child, for her heart yearned over it. That child was Twala. I am his brother born of another wife."

"Well?"

"When Kafa our father died, my brother Imotu was made king in his place. He, too, had a son and his son was called Ignosi was his name. When his son was three years old, Imotu was wounded in battle. It was then that Gagool, the wise and terrible woman who does not die, led out Twala, whom she had hidden among the caves and rocks since he was born and whom she had marked with the sign of the snake—the sign with which the king's eldest son is marked at birth. Before all the people she cried out in a loud voice: 'Behold your king, whom I have saved for you to this day!'"

"Why didn't the people stand by Imotu?" I asked.

"Lord, they go in terror of Gagool. In their fear they cried out 'The King! The King!'

"Hearing their shouts, Imotu crawled from his hut asking 'What is this noise? *I* am your king!'

"Then Twala, his brother, ran to him and took him by the hair and stabbed him through the heart, crying 'No! *I* am the king!' And all the people clapped their hands and cried: 'Twala is king!' So it has been, my lord, until this day."

"And what became of Imotu's wife and her son, Ignosi? Did Twala kill them too?"

"No, my lord. When she saw that her husband was dead, she seized the child and ran away. Two days afterwards she came to a kraal, very hungry, and none would give her food. But at nightfall a little child, a girl, crept out and brought her corn to eat, and she blessed the child, and went on towards the mountains with her boy. There she must have died, for no one has seen her since, nor the child Ignosi."

"Then if this child Ignosi had lived, he would be the true king of the Kukuana people?"

"That is so, my lord; the sacred snake is round his middle. If he lives, he is the king; but alas! he is long dead."

I turned round at that moment to speak to Good, and bumped into Umbopa, who was walking just behind me, listening with great interest to my talk with Infadoos. The expression on his face was most curious, as if he were trying to recall something long forgotten.

For two days more we travelled along Solomon's Road, which ran right into the heart of Kukuanaland. At sunset on the second day we stopped to rest on some high ground, and there on a wide plain before us was Loo itself, the principal place of Twala the king. It was a huge place, quite five miles round, with outlying kraals, and a curious horseshoe-shaped hill about two miles to the north. Sixty or seventy miles away three great snow-capped mountains started up out of the level plain.

In an hour's time we were at the outskirts of the town, which was mapped out by thousands of camp fires. For nearly half an hour we walked through the central street of the great grass town, past endless lines of dome-shaped huts, till Infadoos halted before a hut larger than most. This, he told us, was to be ours.

We entered and found beds made of tanned skins spread upon mattresses of fresh grass. Food, too, was ready for us, and as soon as we had washed ourselves with water, which stood ready in earthenware jars, some young women brought us roasted meat and mealie cobs served on wooden platters.

We ate and drank, then flung ourselves down to sleep, quite worn out by our long journey.

When we woke the sun was high in the sky. We had washed and breakfasted when the message came that Twala was ready to see us. We prepared such presents as our slender stock of

goods permitted, namely the Winchester rifle which had been used by poor Ventvögel, and some beads. The rifle and ammunition we would give to Twala, and the beads were for his wives and courtiers. Guided by Infadoos, we then started off, with Umbopa carrying the gifts.

After walking a few hundred yards we came to an immense enclosure. All round the outside fence was a row of huts, the homes of the king's wives. Opposite the gateway was a very large hut, which stood by itself, in which the king lived. All the rest was open ground; that is to say, it would have been open ground had it not been filled by company after company of warriors, a fine sight in their waving plumes, with their spears and ox-hide shields.

Before Twala's hut were placed several stools. On three of these, at a sign from Infadoos, we seated ourselves, Umbopa standing behind us. Infadoos went and stood by the door of the hut. So we waited for ten minutes in a dead silence, closely watched by some eight thousand pairs of eyes. At length the door of the hut opened and a gigantic figure, with a tiger-skin cloak flung over its shoulders, stepped out, followed by the boy Scragga, and what seemed to us to be a withered-up monkey, wrapped in a fur cloak. The figure seated itself upon a stool, Scragga took his stand behind it, and the withered-up monkey crept on all fours into the shade of the hut and squatted down.

Still there was silence.

Then the gigantic figure slipped off the cloak and stood up before us, a truly alarming spectacle. It was that of an enormous man with the ugliest face we had ever seen. His lips were thick, his nose was flat, he had but one gleaming black eye (there was just a hollow in place of the other), and its expression was

cruel and fierce. On his large head he wore a magnificent plume of white ostrich feathers; his body was clad in a shirt of chain armour, whilst round the waist and right knee was the usual band of white oxtails. In his right hand was a huge spear. Round his neck was a thick band of gold, and bound on to his forehead was a single and enormous uncut diamond.

This man, whom we guessed to be Twala, raised the great spear in his hand. Instantly eight thousand spears were raised in answer, and from eight thousand throats rang out the royal salute of *Koom*. Three times this was repeated, and each time the earth shook with the noise.

"Be humble, O people," piped out a thin voice which seemed to come from the monkey in the shade, "it is the king."

"It is the king," boomed out eight thousand throats in answer.

For a moment there was silence again—dead silence. Then it was broken. A soldier on our left dropped his shield, which fell with a clatter. Twala turned his one cold eye in the direction of the noise.

"Come forward, you!" he said, in a voice of thunder.

The warrior stepped out of the line and cringed before his king.

"It was your shield that fell, you awkward dog!" said Twala fiercely. "Would you make a mock of me in the eyes of these strangers? What have you to say?"

"It was by chance, O lord king," the warrior murmured.

"Then it was a sorry chance, for which you must pay," Twala roared. "Prepare for death!"

"I am the king's ox," was the low answer.

"Scragga," roared the king, "let us see how you can use your spear. Kill me this awkward dog."

Scragga stepped forward with an ugly grin and lifted his spear. The poor victim covered his eyes with his hand and stood still. As for us, we waited, frozen with horror.

Chapter Nine

Gagool the Old

Once, twice, Scragga waved the spear, and then he struck right home—the spear stood out a foot behind the warrior's back! He flung up his arms and dropped dead. A murmur from the crowd rolled round and round, and died away. The thing was finished. Sir Henry sprang up and swore a great oath.

"It was a good thrust," said the king. "Take him away."

Four men stepped out of the ranks and carried away the body of the murdered man.

"Cover up the bloodstains, cover them up," piped out the thin voice from the monkey-like figure; "the king's word is spoken, the king's doom is done."

A girl came from behind the hut, bearing a jar filled with powdered lime, which she scattered over the red marks on the ground.

Sir Henry, meanwhile, was boiling with rage.

"Sit down, for heaven's sake," I whispered; "our lives depend on it."

He yielded and sat down. Twala waited until the traces of the tragedy had been removed, then spoke to us.

"Greeting, white people," he said.

I rose and answered, "Greeting Twala, King of the Kukuanas."

"From whence do you come, white men? What do you seek?"

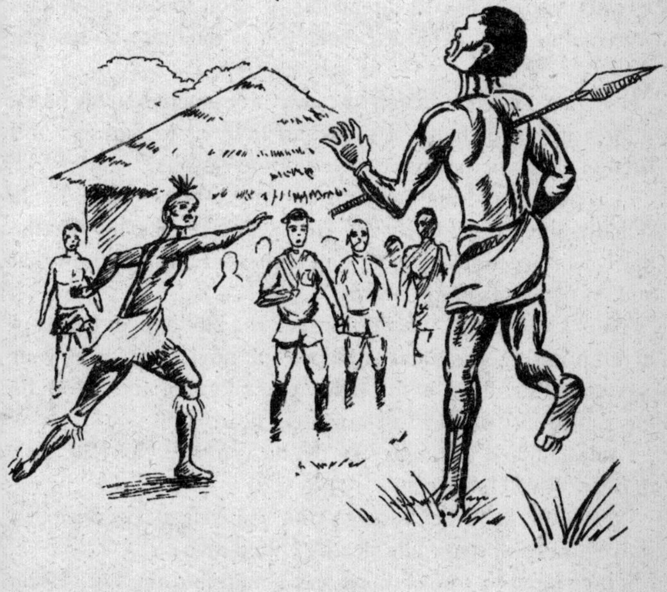

"We come from the stars to see this land."

"You have come far to see a little thing. And that man with you," pointing to Umbopa, "is he too from 'the stars'?"

"Even so. There are people of your colour in the heavens above. But be warned, O king, not to ask of matters that are too high for your understanding."

Twala leaned forward threateningly. "You speak with a loud voice, white man. What if I make you as the one who has just died?"

I laughed out loud, though there was little laughter in my heart.

"Be careful, O king," I said, and pointed to Scragga and Infadoos. "Have they not told you of our powers?"

"They have told me how you kill with a noise," said Twala sullenly, "but I do not believe." He waved a careless hand at the lines of his warriors. 'Kill me a man there and I shall know that you do not speak empty words."

"No," I answered. "We do not shed the blood of men except in just punishment. If you would see our magic, then order your servants to drive an ox through the kraal gates, and before he has run twenty paces I will strike him dead."

Twala laughed jeeringly. "An ox, do you say? No! Kill me a man and I will believe."

"Very well, then. Let Scragga your son walk across this open space and I will strike him dead." I lifted my rifle.

Scragga gave a sort of howl and bolted into the hut. Twala frowned heavily, then called to the two nearest warriors: "Let a young ox be driven in."

The two men departed, running swiftly. I turned to Curtis.

"They're going to drive in an ox," I told him. "I've said that we shall kill it, and I want you to do the shooting this time. I

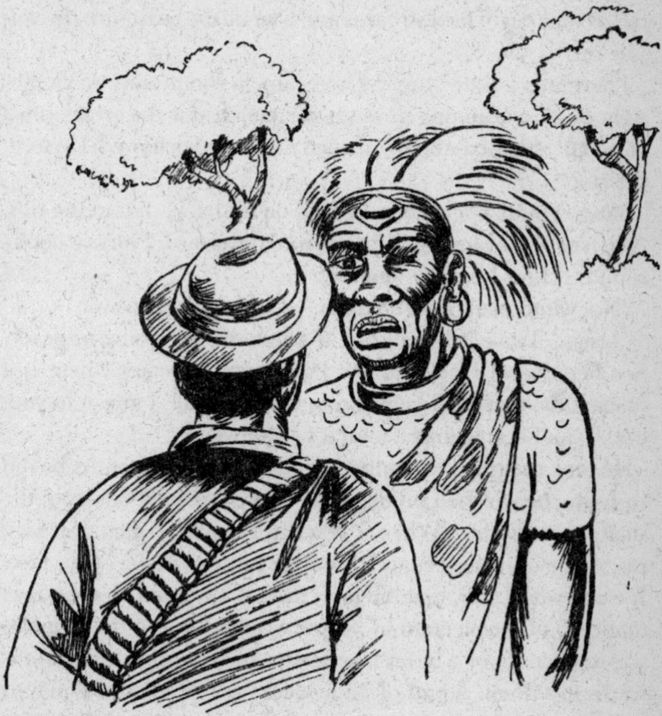

want this ruffian to see that I'm not the only magician of the party."

Sir Henry took up the express rifle and made ready.

"If you miss with the first barrel," I said, "then let him have the second. Sight for 150 yards and wait till the beast turns broadside on."

There was a little pause. Then came a shout, and we caught sight of an ox running through the gate. It saw the great crowd of people, stopped stupidly, turned round and bellowed. Up went the rifle.

Bang! Thud! The ox was kicking on his back, shot in the ribs. A sigh of astonishment went up from the crowd. I turned coolly round, "Have I lied, O king?"

"No, white man, it is the truth," was the awed answer.

"Listen, Twala," I went on, "I know that we come in peace. See here," and I held up the Winchester repeater, "here is a magic tube that shall help you to kill as we kill. I give it to you, but if you lift it against a man it will kill you."

He took the rifle very gingerly and laid it at his feet. As he did so I saw the wizened monkey-like figure creeping out from the shadow of the hut. When it reached the place where the king sat, it rose upon its feet and threw the furry covering off its face. It was a weird and dreadful face: that of a woman of great age, made up of a collection of yellow wrinkles. Set in the wrinkles was a sullen slit of a mouth, beneath which the chin curved outwards to a point. A pair of large black eyes gleamed and played under snow-white eyebrows. The skull was bare and yellow, and its wrinkled scalp moved and contracted like the hood of a cobra.

A shiver of fear passed through me. The old woman began to speak in a thin, shrill voice.

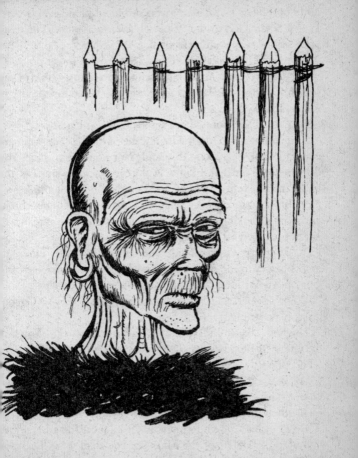

"Listen, O king! Listen, O warriors! The spirit of life is in m
and I prophecy! *Blood! blood!* rivers of blood! Blood everywhere
I see it, I smell it, I taste it! *Footsteps! footsteps! footsteps!* The trea
of the white man coming from afar."

She turned her bald vulture-head towards us, finger pointing

"What do you seek in this land, white men of the stars? Do yo
search for a lost one? He is not here. You come for the brigh
stones. I know it, I know it!"

She turned and pointed her skinny finger at Umbopa.

"And you, with the dark skin and the proud bearing; who ar
you and what seek you in this land? Not stones that shine! Yo
did not come for that. I know you! I can smell the smell of the
blood in your veins. Strip off the skin that hides, that hides—'
Here this strange creature staggered, a hand went to her throa
and, with a choking noise, she fell to the ground foaming in a fi
and was carried off into the hut.

The king rose up trembling, and waved his hand. The regi
ments began to file off. In ten minutes, save for ourselves, the
king, and a few attendants, the great space was left clear.

"White people," said Twala, "it is in my heart to kill you. Gagoo
has spoken strange words."

I laughed. "Be careful, O king. We are not easy to kill. You saw
the fate of the ox. Beware the magic tube that speaks."

The king frowned. "It is not well to threaten a king."

"We do not threaten. We speak only what is true. Try to kill us
O king, and learn."

The great man put a hand to his forehead.

"Go in peace," he said at length. "Tonight is the great witch
hunt and the Dance of the Maidens. You shall see it. Fear no
that I shall set a snare for you. Tomorrow I shall think."

"It is well, O king," I answered carelessly.

The king turned into his hut and Infadoos signalled to us to follow him. When we reached the gate of the kraal, I turned, for some reason, and looked back. I saw that Umbopa was still standing before the king's hut, staring at it. As I watched, he raised his fist and shook it in a threatening gesture. He turned then and walked towards us, and we went back to our hut.

Chapter Ten

Ignosi Returns

On reaching our hut, I asked Infadoos to enter with us.

"It seems to us," I said, "that Twala is a cruel man."

"That is so, my lords. Tonight you will see. It is the great witch hunt and many will be killed. The land groans at the cruelties of Twala."

"Then why is it that the people do not cast him down?"

"If he were killed, Scragga would reign in his place, and the heart of Scragga is blacker than the heart of Twala. If Imotu had never been slain, or if Ignosi, his son, had lived, it would have been otherwise; but they are both dead."

"How do you know that Ignosi is dead?" said a voice behind us. We looked round with astonishment to see who spoke. It was Umbopa.

"What do you mean, boy?" asked Infadoos. "Who told you to speak?"

"Listen, Infadoos," was the answer, "I will tell you a story. The wife of Imotu fled from this land and took the boy Ignosi with

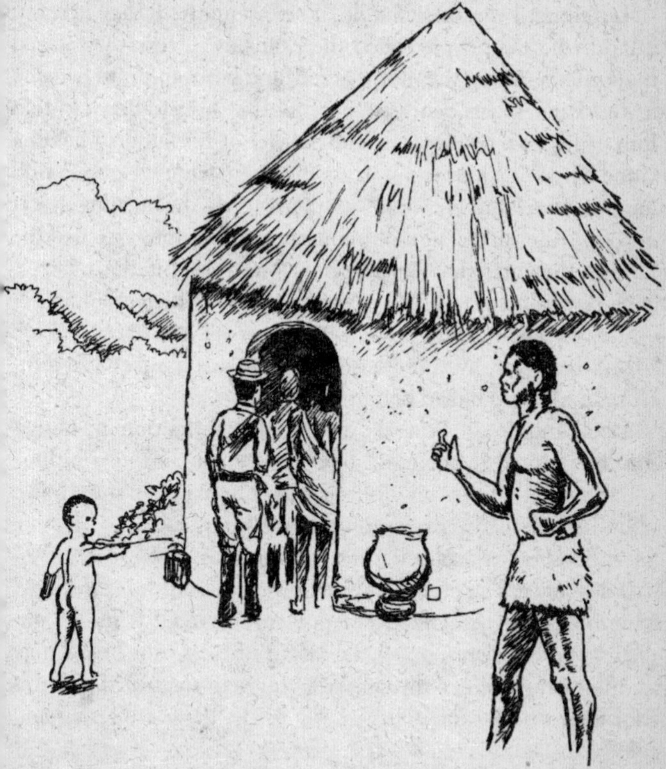

her. They did not die. They crossed the mountains and were led by a tribe of wandering desert men across the sands beyond."

"How do you know this, boy?"

"Listen, and you shall be told. They went on till they reached a land where a people called the Zulus live. Here they stayed many years. At last the mother died, and her son Ignosi became a wanderer. In his heart, he held all that his mother had told him of his own country and the murder of his father. The time came when he met certain white men who were seeking to find an unknown land. He went with them across the burning desert and over the snowclad mountains, and at last they reached the land of the Kukuanas—where they found *you*, Infadoos."

"Surely, you are mad!" said the astonished old gentleman.

"No, my uncle! I will show you. See—*I am Ignosi!*"

With one swift movement he threw off his blanket and loincloth, and stood naked before us.

"Look, Infadoos," he said, "and see the mark upon my body," and he pointed to the mark of a great snake tattooed in blue round his middle, its tail disappearing into its open mouth just above where the thighs are set into the body.

Infadoos looked, started, then fell upon his knees.

"*Koom! Koom!*" he cried. "It is my brother's son! It is the king!"

Umbopa—or rather Ignosi—put out a hand. "Rise, my uncle," he said. "I am not yet the king, but with your help I may win back my father's throne. Will you help me overthrow this murderer and tyrant? Choose, my uncle, between Twala and me."

The old man stood and placed a hand on Ignosi's shoulder.

"You are my rightful king," he said. "I am ready to fight for you against Twala."

"If I conquer, then you shall be the greatest man in my kingdom. "Ignosi turned to us." And you, white men—will you help me?"

As briefly as I could, I explained the situation to Curtis and Good. Then I turned back to Ignosi. "My friends and I will help you," I told him. "Now, you are king by right, but how will you become king indeed?"

"I know not," Ignosi said. "Infadoos, have you a plan?"

"Tonight, lord king," said his uncle, "is the great dance and witch hunt. Many will be smelled out and killed as witches. In the hearts of the people there will be anger against Twala. I will call the great chiefs to you. If you can win them over, you will have twenty thousand spears at your command. But, lord, you must give them a sign that all may know you for their king."

"You have the sign of the snake," Ignosi answered.

"That mark might have been placed there since you came to manhood. They will not move without a sign."

"They shall have their sign, Infadoos," I said. "Go now and call the chiefs to Ignosi, their king."

"As you say, my lord," the old man said, and went from the hut.

Quickly I told Curtis and Good what was needed. Good nodded solemnly.

"I think I have it," he said. Going to a little box in which he kept medicine and things, he unlocked it, and took out a notebook, in the front of which was an almanac. He opened the notebook. "Now, look here, you fellows, today is the fourth of June."

"What of it?" demanded Curtis.

"Ah, here we have it," and he read slowly from the little book.

"*June fourth: total eclipse of the moon begins at eight-fifteen Greenwich time—visible in Tenerife, South Africa, etc.* There's a sign for you!"

"He's got it, by heavens!" cried Curtis. "It's a magnificent idea. He slapped Good on the back. "Good, you're a genius!"

"Thanks, old man," Good said. "You may be right. All you have to do, Quatermain, is to tell them that tonight we shall darken the moon. I'll give you the exact time, if you like."

"It had better be the right time," I said grimly, "or it'll be up with us."

"Here you are," said Good. "I've worked out the reckoning as well as I can. The eclipse will begin here about ten tonight and last until half-past twelve."

"We'll have to risk it," Curtis said. "It's a wonderful idea."

I agreed, and turned to Ignosi. "Tonight, Ignosi," I said, "we shall cause the moon to be eaten up and darkness to cover all the land."

He seemed much impressed. "My friend," he asked, "can you do this wonderful thing?"

"Yes—we think it may be done."

"It is hard to believe, but I know that you do not speak empty words. If you do as you say—and we live through this night—be sure that I shall repay you."

We were interrupted at this moment by the cry that messengers had come from the king. Three men entered, each bearing a shining shirt of chain armour and a magnificent battle-axe.

"The gifts of my lord the king to the white men from the stars," said one of the men.

"We thank the king," I answered. "Leave us."

The men went, and we examined the armour with great interest. It was the most beautiful chainwork we had ever seen.

whole coat fell together so closely that it formed a mass of links almost too big to be covered with both hands.

A second cry at the door told of the return of Infadoos, who entered with some half-dozen stately-looking chiefs.

Ignosi stripped himself again and showed the chiefs the sign of the snake tattooed around him. Then he told them the story we had heard.

"Now you have heard, and you have seen the sign of the snake on this man's body," said Infadoos when he had done. "Speak now; will you stand by this man and help him to his father's throne?"

The eldest of the chiefs, a thickset warrior with white hair, stepped forward a pace and answered: "The land cries out against Twala, but this is a great matter. We may lift our spears for a cheat and a liar. If he is indeed the rightful king, let these white men give us a sign. We will not move without it."

The others murmured their agreement. I stepped forward.

"Tell me, O chiefs," I said, "can any man blow out the moon and bring a curtain of darkness upon the land?"

The chiefs laughed, "No, my lord."

"I tell you that tonight we will cause the moon to be eaten up. A deep darkness shall cover the earth, and you shall know it for a sign that Ignosi is indeed the rightful king of the Kukuanas. If we do this thing, will you be satisfied?"

"Yes, my lord," they answered; "we will be satisfied."

"Two miles from Loo," Infadoos said, "there is a hill curved like the new moon. If my lords can indeed darken the moon, in the darkness I will go to that hill with my regiment and three other regiments which these men command, and thence we can make war on Twala the king."

"It is good," said I. "Now leave us to rest awhile and to make ready our magic."

The chiefs saluted and departed. Infadoos waited a moment and pointed to our chain-mail shirts.

"We know not who made them," he told me, "and there are but few left. He who wears them is well-nigh safe in the battle. The king is well pleased or much afraid, or he would not have sent them. Wear them tonight, my lords."

I told the others what he had said. We all thought it good advice.

Chapter Eleven
The Witch Hunt

The rest of the day we spent resting and talking over the situation, which was sufficiently exciting. At last the sun went down, the watchfires glowed out, and through the darkness we heard the tramp of many feet as the regiments marched to the kraal of the king.

About eight the full moon came up and, as we stood watching it, Infadoos arrived with a guard of twenty men to escort us to the king. We had already put on the shirts of chain armour, wearing them under our ordinary clothing, and finding that they were neither heavy nor uncomfortable. Then, strapping our revolvers round our waists, and taking the battle-axes which the king had sent, we set out.

We found the great kraal closely packed with some twenty thousand men arranged in regiments round it. The regiments were

divided into companies and between each company was a little path to allow free passage to the witch finders to pass up and down. The warriors stood in perfect silence, and the moon poured her light upon the forest of their raised spears and their waving plumes.

"They are very silent," I remarked.

"Those over whom the shadow of death is hovering are silent," answered Infadoos grimly.

"Will many be killed?"

"Very many."

"And are we in danger?"

"I know not, my lord—but do not seem afraid. If we live through the night all may go well."

All this time we had been walking towards the centre of the open space, where stools had been placed. As we went we saw another small party coming from the royal hut.

"It is the king, Twala, and Scragga his son, and Gagool the old, and see, with them are those who slay," said Infadoos pointing to a little group of about a dozen gigantic and savage-looking men, armed with spears in one hand and heavy clubs in the other.

The king seated himself upon the centre stool, Gagool crouched at his feet, and the others stood behind.

"Greeting, white lords," he cried as we came up. "Be seated. Let us not waste time—the moon is high, and the night too short for the deeds that must be done. Begin, Gagool, smeller-out of witches."

"Begin! Begin!" cried out Gagool in her thin voice. "The hyenas howl for food. Begin!"

The king lifted his spear and suddenly twenty thousand pairs

of feet were raised and brought down with a stamp upon the earth. This was done three times, making the ground shake and tremble. Then from a far point of the circle a single voice began a wailing song, starting with the words: "*What is the lot of man born of woman?*"

Back came the answer rolling out from every throat in that great crowd: "*Death!*"

Gradually the song was taken up by company after company, till the whole army was singing it, and I could no longer follow the words. It ended suddenly in one long, heartbreaking wail that went echoing and rolling away. Silence fell. It was broken by a pattering of feet, as from out of the lines of warriors strange and awful figures came running towards us. These were women, ten of them, and most of them aged, for their white hair streamed out behind them. Their faces were painted in stripes of white and yellow; down their backs hung snake skins, and round their waists rattled circlets of human bones, while each held in her hand a small forked wand. They halted in front of us and one of them pointed with her wand towards the crouching figure of Gagool.

"Mother, we are here," she cried.

"Good! Good! Good!" piped out Gagool. "Well, my daughters, are your eyes keen?"

"Mother, they are keen."

"Are your ears open, my daughters? Can you smell blood? Can you rid this land of the wicked ones who plot against the king?"

"Mother, we can."

"Then go, my daughters—the white men from the stars are hungry to see. Go, my daughters, go! Smell out the wicked ones!"

With a wild yell the weird party broke and began to prance towards the lines of warriors. I watched the nearest old woman. When she came within a few paces of the warriors she halted, dancing wildly, and shrieking: "I smell him, the evildoer! I hear the thoughts of him who thought evil of the king!"

She stopped dead all at once, stiffening like a pointer dog when he scents game, and then with outstretched wand began to creep stealthily towards the soldiers before her. It seemed to me that as she came they shrank away from her.

Suddenly the end came. With a shriek she sprang in and touched a tall warrior with the forked wand. At once the warriors on either side of the doomed soldier seized him, and his spear fell from his fingers as they dragged him towards the king. As he came, two of the executioners stepped forward to meet him, then turned towards Twala as though for orders.

"*Kill!*" said the king.

"*Kill!*" squeaked Gagool.

"*Kill!*" said Scragga, with a chuckle.

The thing was done almost before the words were spoken. One man drove his spear into the victim's heart, and the other dashed out his brains with his great club.

"*One*" counted Twala, and the body was dragged away and stretched out.

Hardly was this done, before another victim fell dead.

"*Two,*" counted the king.

And so the deadly game went on till some hundreds of bodies were stretched in rows behind us. We were sickened and once we rose to protest, but were sternly told by Twala: "These dogs are evildoers; it is well that they should die. Let the law take its course, white men."

We had no choice but to sit again upon our stools until, about half-past ten, there was a pause. Then, of a sudden, Gagool rose and, leaning on a stick, slowly hobbled towards us.

"Hang me! She's going to try her tricks on us!" I heard Good say.

I put my hand on my revolver. "You're right," I said. "She's out for our blood!"

Chapter Twelve

Dance of the Maidens

My heart sank into my boots as Gagool drew closer. I glanced behind us at the long rows of corpses and shivered.

Closer and closer she came, her horrid eyes gleaming and glowing in the moonlight. At last she stood still and pointed.

"Which is it to be?" I heard Sir Henry ask.

In a moment we knew. She rushed in and touched Ignosi on the shoulder.

"I smell him out," she shrieked. "Kill him, the stranger, before blood flows for him. Kill him, O king."

I kicked back my stool and came to my feet. "He shall not die, O king," I called out. "This man has our protection."

"Gagool has smelt him out," was the sullen answer. "He must die, white man."

I lifted my revolver. "I will strike dead any man who lays hands on him," I said quietly.

"Seize him," Twala roared.

Two of the executioners started forward. Sir Henry and Good

were on their feet, Sir Henry pointing his revolver at the leading executioner, while Good took aim at Gagool.

Twala winced as my barrel came in a line with his broad chest. The executioners came to a halt.

"Well," I said, "what is it to be, Twala?"

"Put away your magic tubes," he said sullenly. "So be it, white men. The black one shall live. He is lucky, that one—if Gagool had her way he would now be dead."

"I can kill you before you can kill me, O king," said Ignosi calmly.

Twala started. "You speak boldly, white man's dog," he said angrily.

"He may well be bold, who speaks the truth," Ignosi replied. "It is a message from the stars, O king!"

Twala scowled, and his one eye gleamed fiercely, but he said nothing more.

"We are weary of killing," I told Twala. "We were promised other, more pleasant things. We came to see the Dance of the Maidens."

Twala shrugged. "It is well," he said. "Let the dance begin." He pointed to the rows of corpses. "Let these dogs be flung out to the hyenas and the vultures."

It was quickly done. We sat down and waited. Soon two hidden drums began to beat and tap very softly, and a large number of girls, each one crowned with a wreath of flowers, writhed and twisted into sight and advanced into the open space. On they danced in the light of the moon, coming forward and then falling back, while the drums beat louder and faster. At last the dancers paused and stood back, beating time with their hands, while a beautiful young woman sprang out of their line and

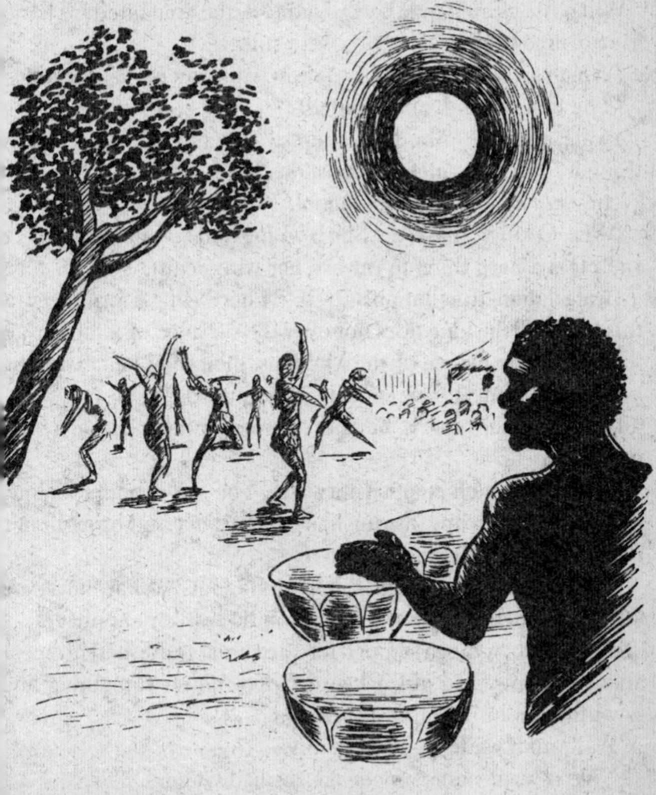

began to dance alone; at length she stood back and another took her place, then another and another, but none of them was as lovely as the first.

When the chosen girls had all danced, the king lifted his hand. The drums stopped; the girls were still.

"Which girl seems to you the fairest, white men?" Twala asked.

"The first," I said, and pointed.

Twala nodded. "She is the fairest," he agreed, "and a sorry thing it is for her, since she must die."

"Aye, must die!" piped out Gagool.

"Why, O king?" I asked. "She is young and fair and has danced well. It is a hard thing to reward her with death."

Twala laughed as he answered, "There runs a prophecy in this land: 'If the king does not offer the sacrifice of a fair girl on the day of the Dance of the Maidens, then shall he fall and his house with him.' I have spoken—she must die."

Turning to the guards, he said, "Bring her here. Scragga, take up your spear."

Two of the men stepped forward. The girl screamed aloud and turned to escape. Strong hands seized her and brought her, struggling and weeping, before us.

"What is your name, girl?" piped Gagool. "What, have you lost your tongue? Shall the king's son do his work at once?"

At this hint, Scragga stepped forward and brandished his spear above the cowering girl. I heard Good mutter something and saw him aim his revolver at Scragga.

"Wait, man wait!" I said urgently.

"Give us your name, my dear," shrilled Gagool.

"My name is Foulata." The girl's voice was trembling. "Why must I die? I have done no wrong."

"It is better to die than to live," answered the evil old hag "when death comes by the hand of the king's son."

"No, mother—no!" the girl cried.

Good gave a snort and stepped forward.

"Look here, you black devils," he cried, "I don't know wha you're saying, but you're not going to harm that girl."

All eyes turned to him. With a quick movement the girl tore herself free and threw herself at his feet.

"Save me, white father from the stars!" she cried.

"Don't worry, old dear," Good sang out. "I'll look after you."

Twala turned and motioned to his son, who advanced with his spear lifted.

"Now's your time," whispered Sir Henry to me. "What are you waiting for?"

"The eclipse," I answered. "There's no sign of it yet."

"Risk it, man—or the girl will be killed."

I stepped between Scragga and the girl.

"Listen, Twala," I said, "this shall not be. Let the girl go in safety."

Twala sprang up. "*Shall not be!*" he roared. "Does the white dog yap at the lion? Scragga, kill her! Guards! Seize these men."

Armed men came running from behind the hut. Sir Henry, Good, and Ignosi ranged themselves alongside of me and lifted their rifles.

"Stop!" I shouted boldly, though my heart was in my boots. "Come one step nearer and we will put out the moon. Remember that we come from the heavens and dwell in her house. Dare to disobey and you shall taste our magic, indeed."

For the moment my threat worked. The men halted and Scragga stood still before us.

"Hear him!" piped Gagool. "Hear the liar who says he will put out the moon like a lamp. Let him do it and the girl shall be spared. Yes, I say, let him do it—or die with the girl!"

I glanced at the moon and saw, to my great joy, that we had made no mistake. On the edge of the great disc was a faint rim of shadow, while a smoky hue grew and gathered on its bright surface.

I lifted a hand towards the sky, and at once Curtis and Good did the same.

"Listen, O people," I cried, "to the magic words that shall put out the light of the moon." And then, in English and in a slow, deep voice, I began to recite "Humpty Dumpty".

The light dimmed as I did so. A gasp of fear went up.

"It's working, Curtis," I cried. "Come on, back me up. And you, Good."

Sir Henry began to declaim some lines from Shakespeare, while Good, with outstretched arms, raised his face to the sky and began to sing "Rule Britannia".

Our "magic" was working. The light was fading fast. A groan of terror rose from the onlookers. They shouted and wailed, and some fell to their knees.

"See, Twala!" I cried. "Look, Gagool! Behold, chiefs and warriors, and see if the white men are empty liars!"

"It is a cloud!" screeched Gagool. "It will pass!"

"It will not pass," I shouted at her. "See how the moon grows black before your eyes."

I turned to the warriors, "You have asked for a sign; we have given it to you. Grow dark, O moon, grow darker yet!"

It did so. On crept the ring of darkness until we could hardly see the fierce faces of the group before us. And still Curtis and

Good shouted and sang at the sky, while the Kukuanas shrieked and howled.

"The moon is dying!" yelled Scragga. "We shall perish in the dark!"

He leaped towards us and drove his spear at Sir Henry's broad chest. The steel rebounded from the mail shirt that Curtis wore, and then Sir Henry snatched it from his hand and sent it straight through him. He dropped dead.

Then came panic. The companies of warriors turned away and ran; the dancing girls tore screeching towards the gateways. The king himself, followed by his guards, and Gagool, hobbling after them, fled for the huts. In a minute or so we were left with Foulata, Infadoos, and most of the chiefs with whom we had talked earlier, together with the dead body of Scragga.

"Chiefs," I said, "we have given you the sign. Come now, and let us fly quickly to the place you spoke of."

Infadoos stepped forward. "Behold your king," he said and pointed to Ignosi.

"Look upon my face," Ignosi called to the chiefs. "My name is Ignosi—I am the son of Imotu and, by right of blood, I am your king. I say to you, I am your king!"

He lifted his battle-axe above his head. The chiefs called out his name in wonder.

"Come," said Infadoos, turning to go, and was followed by the awed chiefs, ourselves, and the girl Foulata, whom Good took by the hand.

Before we reached the gate of the kraal the moon went out, and the stars seemed to rush into the inky sky.

Holding each other by the hand we stumbled on through the darkness.

Chapter Thirteen
Before the Battle

Infadoos and the chiefs knew all the pathways of the town and so, even in the gloom, we made fair progress.

After little more than an hour the eclipse began to pass. That edge of the moon which had first disappeared again became visible. Suddenly there burst from it a silver streak of light, and with it a red glow, which hung upon the blackness of the sky like a great lamp, and a wild and lovely sight it was. Within minutes the stars began to fade and we saw that we were well clear of the town of Loo and making for a large, flat-topped hill, shaped like a horseshoe. On the flat grassland at the top was a camping ground. Here we found crowds of men, huddled together, shivering with fright at the strange thing they had seen.

We passed through them until we came to a hut in the centre of the ground, where we were astonished to find two men waiting with all our belongings.

"I sent for them," Infadoos told us, "also for these" and he lifted up Good's long-lost trousers.

With a cry of joy, Good sprang up and began to pull them on.

"Surely my lord will not hide his beautiful white legs!" said Infadoos, regretfully, but Good paid no regard to that.

At sunrise the troops—nearly twenty thousand men in all—were mustered, and Ignosi spoke to them. He told them the story of his father, murdered by Twala the king, and of the wife and child driven out to starve.

"That I am indeed the king," he ended, "your chiefs can te
you, for they have seen the snake about my middle. They aske
for a sign, and the white lords from the stars have given them
sign. I am the king" and he drew himself to his full height, lif
ing his battle-axe above his head. "If there be any man amon
you who says that it is not so, let him stand forth and I will figh
him now. Let him stand forth, I say!" and he shook the great ax
till it flashed in the sunlight.

No man stepped forward.

"I am indeed the king, and if I win the day you shall be the fir
of my warriors in this land. And I will give you justice. Have yo
chosen, chiefs and warriors?"

"We have chosen, O king," was the answer.

"It is well. Tomorrow, Twala will come with all who are faith
ful to him. Then shall I see the man who is indeed my man
Now make you ready for war."

The warriors marched off, and we held a council of war wit
the chiefs. From the hill we could see messengers going out fro
Loo in all directions, to summon regiments to fight for Twala
He would have, the chiefs thought, about thirty-five thousan
men, but they were sure that no attack would be made that da
It would come tomorrow, they said, and they proved to be righ

Just before sundown a small party of men came from Loo, on
of them carrying a palm leaf as a sign that he was a herald. W
went with Ignosi and some of the chiefs to the foot of the hill t
meet him, a fine-looking fellow in a leopard-skin cloak.

"Greeting!" he cried as he came near, "The lion's greeting t
the jackals who snarl round his heels."

"Speak," I said.

"These are the words of Twala, the one-eyed, the mighty: '

will have mercy and be satisfied with little blood. One in every ten shall die, the rest shall go free; but the white man Incubu who slew Scragga my son, and the black man, his servant, who pretends to my throne, and Infadoos, who brews rebellion against me, these shall die by torture.' Such are the merciful words of Twala."

I answered him in a loud voice, so that our soldiers might hear: "Go back, you dog, and say that all who are gathered here make this answer: 'We will not surrender; before the sun has twice gone down Twala's corpse shall stiffen at Twala's gate, and Ignosi, whose father Twala slew, shall reign in his place." Now go, dog, before we whip you away."

The herald laughed. "Show yourselves as bold tomorrow, O white men who darken the moon. Perhaps we may meet in the fight; wait for me, I pray, white men." And with this he went, and almost at once the sun sank.

There was nothing more we could do. We ate some food and then slept as best we could.

Just about dawn we were awakened by Infadoos, who came to say that parties of the king's skirmishers were making for our outposts.

We dressed ourselves for the battle, each putting on his chain-armour shirt. Sir Henry went the whole way and dressed himself like a Kukuana chief, for Infadoos had provided him with a set of war uniform. He wore a leopard-skin cloak, and a plume of black ostrich feathers. He had a heavy battle-axe, a round iron shield covered with white ox hide, a set of throwing knives, and, to these, he added his revolver. When Ignosi arrived dressed in his war uniform, I thought to myself that I had never seen two finer-looking men.

We hastily swallowed some food, then started out to see how things were going. At one point there was a little koppie of stone, and here we found Infadoos surrounded by his regiment, the Greys, the finest in the Kukuana army, which was to be held in reserve. The men were lying on the grass and watching the king's forces creep out of Loo in long, ant-like columns. There seemed to be no end to these columns, three in all, and each numbering at least eleven or twelve thousand men.

As soon as they were clear of the town, one column marched off to the right, one to the left, and the third came slowly on towards us.

"Ah," said Infadoos, "they are going to attack us on three sides at once."

And so, indeed, it proved. Slowly the three columns crept on. When within about five hundred yards of us, the centre one came to a halt, waiting for the other two to move into position.

"Oh, for a machine gun," groaned Good. "I would clear the plain in twenty minutes."

"We don't have one," said Curtis, "but suppose you try a shot, Quatermain. See how near you can get to that tall fellow who seems to be in command. Two to one in sovereigns that you miss him."

This annoyed me, so I loaded the express rifle, then lay down and rested it upon a rock to steady it. I waited till my target walked some ten yards out from his force in order to get a better view of our position. I fired, but missed him altogether, whilst his orderly, who was at least three paces to the left, fell to the ground.

"Bravo, Quatermain," sang out Good. "You've frightened him."

This made me angry. I hate to miss in public. I took quick aim and fired again. The poor man threw up his arms and fell forward on his face.

Our warriors cheered wildly at this, while Twala's men began to fall back in confusion. Sir Henry and Good also began to fire, and I had another shot or two, so that we put some eight or ten men out of action before they got out of range.

Just as we stopped firing there came a roar from our far right, and another from our left. They were coming at us from both sides.

Chapter Fourteen

The Attack

As if at a signal the mass of men before us opened out a little, and came on towards the hill at a slow trot, chanting a deep-throated song. We kept up a steady fire from our rifles, and some fell, but on they came with a shout and the clashing of spears. Our first line of defence was about halfway up the hill, our second fifty yards farther back, while our third held the edge of the plain.

On they came shouting their war-cry: *"Twala! Twala! Chielé! Chielé!"* (Twala! Twala! Smite! Smite!).

"Ignosi! Ignosi! Chielé! Chielé!" answered our people.

The enemy were quite close now and throwing knives began to flash backwards and forwards. Then with an awful yell the battle closed in.

To and fro swayed the mass of struggling warriors. By sheer

weight of numbers, the enemy forced back our first line, the our second, till at last our third line came into action.

By this time the enemy were much exhausted, and had lo many men. They could not break the thick hedge of spears tha made our line. After watching the desperate struggle for a whil Sir Henry suddenly rushed off, followed by Good, and flun himself into the thick of it. As for myself, I remained where was.

Our soldiers, catching sight of Sir Henry, fought with new hear Inch by inch the attacking force was pressed back down the hill side. Just then we had news that the left attack had been drive off. I nodded happily to myself, thinking the battle nearly ove when to our horror we saw our men on the right being drive towards us across the plain, followed by swarms of the enemy.

Ignosi, who was standing by me, gave an order. Instantly th reserve regiment around us, the Greys, spread out and began t move upon the enemy.

I could do no more than go with them. I put myself behin Ignosi's great body and made the best of a bad job, toddlin along to be killed. In a minute or two it seemed to me that ther were men plunging and flying all round me, and then I am no at all sure what happened. I remember the dreadful noise mad by the clash of spears, wild shrieks and yells, and then all at onc a huge Kukuana, whose eyes seemed to be starting out of hi head, made straight at me with a bloody spear. As he came, threw myself down in front of him so that he took a header ove me. Before he could rise, I was on my knees and shot him wit my revolver.

Soon after this, somebody knocked me down and I remembe no more of the charge.

When I came to I found myself lying on the ground, with Good bending over me.

"How do you feel?" he asked.

I got up and shook myself.

"Pretty well, thank you," I answered.

"Praise be! I thought you were done for."

"Not this time," I told him. "I only got a rap on the head. How has it ended?"

"For the moment we've driven them back, but we've lost at least two thousand men, and they must have lost three."

We went in search of Sir Henry, whom we found with Ignosi, Infadoos and other chiefs, making plans of war.

I was told that Twala, who still commanded a large force, seemed set upon holding us upon our hill until he had starved us out.

"That's awkward," I said.

"Yes—especially as Infadoos says that the water supply has given out."

"We must choose between three things," Infadoos said to me: "to stay here and starve, to break away towards the north, or"—and here he pointed towards the enemy—"to launch ourselves at Twala's throat. What say you, white men from the stars?"

I spoke quickly to Good, Sir Henry, and Ignosi. We were all of the same mind. I turned back to Infadoos.

"We should attack at once," I said, "before our wounds grow stiff."

"I will strike at Twala," Ignosi added, "and this is how it shall be done. You see how the hill curves round like the half-moon, and how the plain runs like a green tongue towards us within the curve?"

"We see," I answered.

"Good; it is now midday and the men eat and rest after the toil of battle. When the sun has turned and travelled a little towards the dark, let our regiment, my uncle, advance with one other down to the green tongue. Twala will hurl his force at it to crush it. But the spot is narrow and the regiments can come against you one at a time only; so shall they be destroyed one by one. With you, my uncle, shall go Incubu; when Twala sees his battle-axe flashing in the first rank of the Greys his heart may grow faint.

I will come with the second regiment, so that if you are destroyed, as it may happen, there may yet be a king left to fight for; and with me shall come Macumazahn the wise."

"It is well, O king," said Infadoos.

"And while the eyes of all Twala's men are fixed upon the fight," went on Ignosi, "one third of the men who are left to us shall creep along the right horn of the hill and fall upon the left flank of Twala's force, and one third shall creep along the left horn and fall upon Twala's right flank. And when I see that the horns are ready to toss Twala, then will I, with the men who are left to me, charge home in Twala's face. And now let us eat and make ready; and stay, let my white father, Bougwan, go with the right horn that his shining eye may give courage to the men."

Within little more than an hour the plan of attack had been explained to the leaders and the whole force, now numbering about eighteen thousand men, was ready to start.

The final battle was about to begin.

Chapter Fifteen
The Last Stand of the Greys

In a few more minutes the two wings of the army tramped off in silence, keeping under the lee of the rising ground to hide their movement from the eyes of Twala's scouts. We were to wait half an hour before any movement was made by the Greys and the supporting regiment, the Buffaloes.

I looked down the long lines of waving black plumes and sighed to think that within one short hour most of these fine warriors would be laid dead or dying in the dust.

Ignosi put himself at the head of the Buffaloes, gave the word to march, and off we went.

By the time we reached the edge of the slope ending in the tongue of grassland, the Greys were already halfway down it. The excitement in Twala's camp on the plain was very great. Regiment after regiment were starting forward at a long swinging trot. The Greys passed down the side of the hill and on to the tip of the tongue and halted there. We took our stand in reserve, about one hundred yards behind, and on slightly higher ground.

Twala's great force moved swiftly towards us, but slowed as they discovered that only one regiment at a time could advance into the gorge. Finally they came to a halt. There was no eagerness to cross spears with those lines of grim warriors who stood so firm and ready. Then Twala himself came running up and gave an order. The first regiment charged up towards the Greys, who

stood still and silent till the attacking troops were within forty yards. Then, with a bound and a roar, they sprang forward with uplifted spears. The two regiments met. To and fro swung the struggling mass, until the attacking lines seemed to grow thinner. Then, with a long, slow heave the Greys passed over them. It was done; that regiment was destroyed, but the Greys had only two lines left now. A third of their number were dead.

They closed up once more and waited for the next charge. I was glad to catch sight of Sir Henry's yellow beard as he moved to and fro among them. He was still alive!

We moved up on to the field of the battle. Four thousand men lay there, dead, dying, and wounded, and it was stained red with blood.

But now a second regiment, wearing white plumes, was charging at the remaining two thousand Greys. Again there came the awful roll of their meeting, but this time the fight lasted longer. Hundreds of men were struck down; there came to my ears shouts and screams and groans, set to the clashing music of meeting spears. Then, above the din, I heard Sir Henry's voice ringing out, and caught sight of his circling battle-axe as he waved it high above his plumes.

There came a change. The Greys stood still as a rock for a time, then moved forward. The attacking regiment fled. Of the three thousand men who had gone into action, there remained at most six hundred blood-bespattered warriors. And yet they cheered and waved their spears, and then ran forward for a hundred yards to take possession of a little knoll of rising ground. I caught a glimpse of Sir Henry on top of the mound before Twala's regiments rolled down upon the doomed band, and once more the battle closed in.

"Are we to stand here till we put out roots, Ignosi?" I asked impatiently.

"No, Macumazahn," was the answer, "see, now is the ripe moment; let us pluck it."

As he spoke, a fresh regiment rushed past the ring upon the mound, and wheeling round, attacked it from our side.

Ignosi lifted his battle-axe and, giving their battle cry, the Buffaloes charged home with a rush like the rush of the sea.

All I can remember is a wild rushing that seemed to shake the ground; a sudden change of front on the part of the regiment before us; then an awful shock, a dull roar of voices, and a mad flashing of spears seen through a red mist of blood. When my mind cleared I found myself standing inside the remnant of the Greys near the top of the mound, and behind Sir Henry himself. How I got there I had no idea.

And still the battle raged. It was a splendid sight to see that sturdy old warrior, Infadoos, shouting orders and even jests to keep up the spirit of his men. But yet more gallant was the sight of Sir Henry, whose ostrich plumes had been shorn off by a spear stroke, so that his long yellow hair streamed out in the breeze behind him. There he stood, the great Viking, for he was nothing else, his hands, his axe, and his armour all red with blood, and none could live before his stroke.

Suddenly there rose a cry of "*Twala, y' Twala*". Out of the press sprang the gigantic one-eyed king, also armed with battle-axe and shield.

"Incubu, thou white dog who slew my son—see if you can kill me!" he shouted, and hurled a knife straight at Sir Henry, who caught it on his shield, where it stayed wedged in the iron plate behind the hide.

Then, with a cry, Twala sprang straight at him, and with his battle-axe struck him such a blow upon the shield that the shock of it brought Sir Henry down upon his knees.

The matter went no further. At that moment there rose from the regiments pressing round us something like a shout of dismay. And then I saw the reason.

To both right and left the plain was alive with the plumes of charging warriors. The outflanking warriors had come to our relief.

In five minutes the battle was decided. Twala's regiments broke into flight and soon the whole plain before Loo was scattered with groups of flying soldiers. The forces that had surrounded us melted away and we were left standing there like a rock from which the sea has retreated. Around us the dead and dying lay in heaped-up masses, and of the gallant Greys there remained alive but ninety-five men.

Infadoos, who was binding up a wound in his arm, looked round at what was left of his Greys.

"Men," he said calmly, "this day's fighting will be spoken of by your children's children." Then he turned round and shook Sir Henry by the hand. "Thou art a great man, Incubu," he said simply. "I have lived a very long life among warriors, yet I have never seen a man like you."

At this moment the Buffaloes began to march past on the road to Loo. A message was brought to us from Ignosi asking that we join him. We did so. He told us that he was pressing on to Loo to complete the victory by capturing Twala, if he could. Before we had gone far we saw Good sitting on an ant-heap about a hundred paces from us. Close beside him was the body of a Kukuana.

"Good must be wounded," said Sir Henry anxiously.

As he spoke, the dead body of the Kukuana soldier, or wha
had seemed to be his dead body suddenly sprang up, knocke
Good head-overheels off the ant-heap and began to stab at hir
with his spear.

Chapter Sixteen
The End of Twala

We rushed forward in terror.

The warrior was making dig after dig at Good. Seeing us com
ing he gave one final stab and fled. When we reached him Goo
did not move, and we were sure that our poor friend was don
for. Sadly we came up to him and were astonished to find hir
faint and pale, but with a smile upon his face, and his eyeglas
still fixed in his eye.

"Splendid armour this," he murmured. "Fooled that chap com
pletely." Then he fainted.

We examined him and found that he had been badly wounde
in the leg by a throwing knife, but that the chain armour ha
stopped his assailant's spear from doing anything more tha
bruise him badly. We placed him on one of the wicker shield
used for the wounded, and carried him along with us.

On arriving before the nearest gate of Loo, we found one o
our regiments watching it, as ordered by Ignosi. The officer i
command told us that Twala's army had taken refuge in th
town. Ignosi sent heralds to each gate ordering the defenders to
open and offering forgiveness to every soldier who laid dow

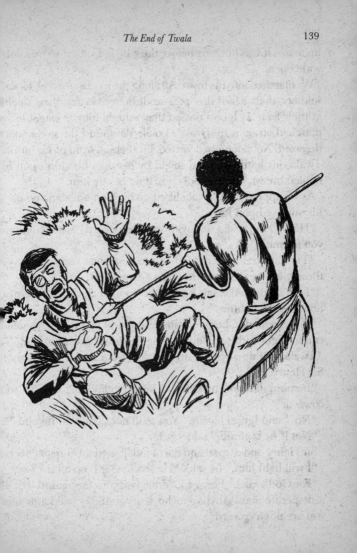

his arms. It was not long before the gate in front of us was flung wide open.

We marched into the town. All along the roadway stood Twala's soldiers, their heads drooping and the spears and their shield at their feet. As Ignosi passed they saluted him as king. On we marched straight to Twala's kraal. We found the great space deserted. No, not quite deserted, for there in front of his hut, sat Twala, his battle-axe and shield by his side, his chin upon his mailed breast, and Gagool crouching beside him.

As we approached, Twala lifted up his plumed head and fixed his one eye upon Ignosi.

"Hail, O king," he said with bitter mockery; "what fate have you for me?"

"The fate you gave my father, whose throne you have sat on these many years!" was the stern answer.

"I am ready to die, but I crave the boon of the Kukuana royal house to die fighting."

"It is granted. Choose—with whom will you fight? Myself I cannot fight with you, for the king fights not except in war."

Twala's sombre eye ran up and down our ranks. It settled on Sir Henry.

"Incubu, shall we end what we began today, or shall I call you coward?"

"No!" said Ignosi hastily. "You shall not fight with Incubu."

"Not if he is afraid," said Twala.

Sir Henry understood and the blood flamed up into his cheeks.

"I will fight him," he said. "He shall see if I am afraid."

"For God's sake," I begged, "don't risk your life against that of a desperate man. Anybody who saw you today will know that you are not a coward."

"I will fight him," was the sullen answer. "I am ready now!" He stepped forward and lifted his axe.

"Fight not, my white brother," begged Ignosi. "You have fought enough."

"I will fight," was Sir Henry's answer.

Twala laughed savagely, stepped forward, and faced Curtis. The setting sun caught their great bodies and clothed them both in fire. They were a well-matched pair. They began to circle round each other, battle-axes raised.

Suddenly Sir Henry sprang forward and struck a fearful blow at Twala, who stepped to side. Sir Henry staggered and almost fell. Twala circled his battle-axe around his head and brought it down with tremendous force. My heart jumped into my mouth, but with a quick upward movement of the left arm Sir Henry thrust his shield between himself and the axe. Its outer edge was shorn clean off, the axe falling on his left shoulder, but not heavily enough to do any serious damage. Sir Henry got in another blow, taken by Twala upon his shield. Then blow followed blow, either received upon the shield or avoided. The excitement grew; the onlookers shouted and groaned at every stroke.

Presently Sir Henry, having caught a fresh stroke upon his shield, hit out with all his force. The stroke cut through Twala's shield and through the chain armour behind it, gashing him in the shoulder. With a yell of pain and fury, he returned the stroke, and cut right through his enemy's axe-handle.

There was a cry of dismay as Curtis's axe-head fell to the ground. Twala flew at him with a shout. I shut my eyes. When I opened them again it was to see Sir Henry's shield lying on the ground, and Sir Henry himself with his great arms twined round Twala's middle. To and fro they swung, then down they came

together, rolling over and over, Twala striking out at Curtis's head with his battle-axe, and Sir Henry trying to drive the knife he had drawn from his belt through Twala's armour.

It was a mighty struggle, and an awful sight.

"Get his axe!" yelled Good; and perhaps our champion heard him.

At any rate, dropping the knife, he made a grab at the axe which was fastened to Twala's wrist by a strip of buffalo hide. Still rolling over and over they fought for it like wild cats. Suddenly the hide string burst and, with a great effort, Sir Henry freed himself, the weapon in his grasp.

Another second and he was up on his feet, blood streaming from a wound in his face. Twala was up, too. Drawing the heavy knife from his belt, he staggered straight at Curtis and struck him upon the breast. The blow was a hard one, but Sir Henry's chain armour withstood the steel. Twala gave a savage yell and struck again; once more the steel rebounded and Sir Henry went staggering back. Twala came on and Sir Henry gathered himself together. He swung the heavy axe round his head and hit at him with all his force. There was a shriek of excitement from a thousand throats. Twala's head seemed to spring from his shoulders and then fell and came rolling and bounding along the ground towards Ignosi, stopping just at his feet. For a second the corpse stood upright, blood spouting from the neck; then with a dull crash it fell to the earth, and the gold chain that Twala had worn went rolling away. As it did so, Sir Henry, overpowered by faintness and loss of blood, fell heavily across it.

He was lifted in a second. Eager hands poured water on his face. Another minute and his eyes opened wide.

He was not dead!

Then, just as the sun sank, I stepped to where Twala's head
lay in the dust, unloosened the diamond from the dead brow
and handed it to Ignosi.

"Take it," I said, "lawful King of the Kukuanas."

He bound the diamond upon his brows and turned to his warriors.

"Rejoice, my people!" he cried. "Tyranny is trodden down
and I am the king!"

Out of the gathering gloom there came back the deep reply
"Thou art the king."

So it was that my words to the herald came true and, with
the forty-eight hours, Twala's headless corpse was stiffening
Twala's gate.

Chapter Seventeen

Good Falls Ill

Sir Henry and Good were carried to our hut, where I joined
them. Both were weak from loss of blood, and my head was
aching badly from the blow I had had in the morning. Somehow, with the help of Foulata, who had made herself our
handmaiden, we managed to get off the chain shirts and found
that Curtis and Good were a mass of bruises.

Foulata brought us a plaster made from pounded green leaves
which gave us some relief, but there was little she could do for
the wounds of my two friends. Good had a hole right through
the fleshy part of his "beautiful white leg", and Sir Henry a
deep cut over the jaw. Luckily Good was a pretty fair surgeon

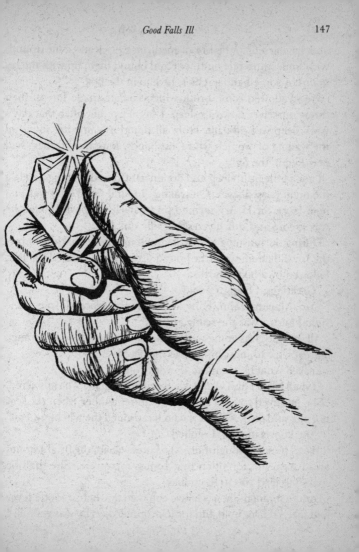

and, having sent for his box of medicines, he cleansed the wounds with some antiseptic ointment and bound them up with the remains of some handkerchiefs he had in the box.

We swallowed some broth which Foulata made for us, then threw ourselves down to sleep. I say sleep; but after that day's work sleep was difficult. From all round us came the sound of the wailing of women whose husbands, sons and brothers had perished in the fight.

I got a little fitful sleep and dreamed of dreadful things. At last the night passed away. On waking, I found that Good was in a high fever. Sir Henry seemed pretty lively in spirit, though he was so sore and stiff he could hardly stir.

During the morning we had a visit from Ignosi, on whose brows the royal diadem was now bound. I rose as he entered the hut, followed by a bodyguard.

"Greetings, O king," I said.

"Yes, Macumazahn. King at last, by the grace of your three right hands," was the ready answer.

All, he said, was going well. In two weeks he hoped to arrange a great feast to show himself to the people.

I asked what he meant to do with Gagool.

"I shall kill her and all the witch-finders with her," he answered. "She has lived so long that none can remember when she was not old, and always she it is who has trained the witchhunters."

"She knows much," I replied.

"Yes," he said thoughtfully, 'she knows where the bright stones are. I have not forgotten that I must repay you. She shall be spared to lead you to the mines."

For the moment, however, we could go nowhere. Good's fever had taken a firm hold and for four or five days he was very ill. I

was sure he was going to die. Sir Henry thought so, too, and we crept about with heavy hearts. Only Foulata, who nursed him day and night would not believe it.

"He will live," she said.

And so, indeed, it proved. On the fifth night his fever left him, and he slept soundly with Foulata's fingers clasped tightly in his hand. The crisis had passed. He slept like that for eighteen hours, and for all that time the poor girl stayed by his side.

He began to recover quickly, but it was not till he was nearly well that Curtis told him all that he owed to Foulata. When he heard he went straight to where Foulata was preparing our midday meal, taking me with him so that he could speak with her.

"Tell her," he said, "that I owe her my life, and that I will never forget her kindness."

I told her, and I'll swear that under her dark skin she actually seemed to blush.

She answered softly, glancing at him with her large brown eyes, "My lord forgets! Did he not save *my* life, and am I not my lord's handmaiden?"

The young lady seemed to have forgotten the part which Sir Henry and myself had played in saving her!

It was a few days after this that Ignosi held his great council and was recognized as king by the head men of Kukuanaland.

Later that day we went to him and told him that we were now ready to investigate the mystery of the mines to which Solomon's Road ran.

"My friends," he said, "there are things I have discovered. Deep in the mountains known as the 'Three Witches', is a great cave where the kings of this land are buried. There, also, is a deep pit, which was dug by men who are long since dead—and there,

too, is a hidden chamber, secret to all save Gagool. It is said that
once, long ago, a white man crossed the mountains and was led
by a woman to the dark chamber and shown the wealth hidden
there. Before he could carry it away, the woman betrayed him
and the king of that time drove him back to the mountains."

"The story is true, Ignosi, for on the mountains we found the
white man."

"Yes, we found him. And now I promise you that if you find
that chamber, and the stones are there—"

"The gem upon your forehead proves that the stones are there,"
I said, pointing to the great diamond I had taken from Twala's
dead brows.

"If they are, you shall have as many as you can carry with you
when you go—if, indeed, you would leave me, my brothers."

"We must find the chamber first," I said.

"Only Gagool can show it to you."

"And if she will not?"

"Then shall she die," said Ignosi sternly. "I have kept her alive
but for this," and calling to a messenger he ordered Gagool to
be brought.

In a few minutes she came, hurried along by two guards.

"Leave her," said the king to the guards.

As they stepped back, the withered old bundle sank into a heap
on the floor, out of which her two bright, wicked eyes gleamed
like a snake's.

"Listen, old witch," Ignosi said, "you must reveal to us the
chamber where the bright stones are hidden."

"Ha, ha!" she piped. "I will never tell you. The white devils
shall go back to the stars with empty hands."

"I will make you tell me, old woman."

"All your power cannot wring the truth from me."

"If you refuse, then you shall die, Gagool."

"Die!" she shrieked in terror and fury. "I cannot die—for non
dare kill me!"

"I will dare, old mother of evil," said Ignosi angrily, and h
seized a spear and held it over her. "You shall see whether th
king dares!"

Slowly he brought down the spear till it pricked the still hea
of rags. With a wild yell she sprang to her feet, and then aga
fell and rolled upon the floor.

"No, no," she screeched, "do not kill me! I will show you th
place. But only the white men may enter the chamber. No ma
of our race shall enter for fear of the curse that shall fall upo
him."

"Tomorrow," Ignosi said, "you shall go with Infadoos and m
white brothers to show them this place of the bright stones. An
beware, Gagool—if you fail, then you shall die. I have spoken

"I will not fail, Ignosi. I always keep my word."

She cackled. "Ah, we shall make a merry journey together—
we can see the bodies of those who died in the battle as we g
Their eyes will be gone by now, and their ribs will be hollow. H
ha, ha!"

Chapter Eighteen
The Place of Death

At dusk, three days later, we camped in some huts at the foot
the triangle of mountains known as the "Three Witches". W

had with us Infadoos, Foulata, Gagool, who was carried in a litter, and a party of guards and attendants.

I can still remember the feeling of excitement with which we set out on our march the next morning. At last we were drawing near to the wonderful mines that had been the cause of the death of the old Portuguese, three centuries before. Should we fare any better?

Straight before us the white ribbon of Solomon's Road stretched away uphill to the foot of the centre peak, about five miles from us, and there stopped.

For an hour and a half we tramped on up the road till we saw between ourselves and the peak a great circular hole with sloping sides, three hundred feet or more in depth, and quite half a mile round.

"Can't you guess what this is?" I said to Sir Henry and Good, who were staring down into this awful pit.

They shook their heads.

"Then you have never seen the diamond mines at Kimberley. This is Solomon's Mine. Do you see that blue clay, there—the watercourse and those slabs of rock? If those aren't tables that were used to wash the 'stuff', then I'm a Dutchman."

At the edge of this vast hole the great road branched into two and went round it. We pressed along it, wanting to find out what were the three towering objects we could see ahead. As we drew near we saw that they were great carvings of stone, the "Silent Ones" held in awe by the Kukuana people.

Each was about twenty feet high. One, in the centre, had a female head; the others were male. All had been given an expression of great cruelty by their unknown sculptor.

Infadoos came up as we stood there and saluted the Silent

Ones by lifting his spear. He asked if we meant to enter th
Place of Death at once, or if we would wait till after we had
eaten at midday. Gagool was willing to guide us now. We none
of us could wait, so I suggested we take some food with us.

Gagool's litter was brought up and the old lady helped out
Foulata put some *biltong* (dried game-flesh) and a couple of gourd
of water into a reed basket, and we set out.

Straight in front of us rose a sheer wall of rock, eighty feet o
more in height. It sloped up till it formed the base of the loft
snow-wreathed peak which soared up three thousand feet abov
us. Gagool gave us an evil grin and then, leaning on a stick
hobbled off towards the face of the rock. We followed her till w
came to a narrow archway that looked like the opening of
mine gallery.

"Now, white men from the stars," piped out Gagool, "make
strong your hearts to bear what you shall see. Come, here is th
lamp," and she drew a gourd full of oil, and fitted with a rush
wick, from under her fur cloak.

Without further ado, she plunged into the dark opening. W
went after her in some fear and trembling, Foulata clutching
Good by the hand. There was the sound of a sudden rush o
wings, and a little scream from Foulata.

"Somebody hit me in the face," said Good.

"Bats," I told him. "On you go."

After another fifty paces the passage grew lighter. Anothe
minute and we stood in the most wonderful place that the eye
of living man ever lit upon.

It was a cave, the size of a cathedral, dimly lighted from above
by shafts driven in the roof.

Running down its length were giant pillars of what looked like

ice, but which, in fact, were huge stalagmites. Some of them were twenty feet round and many sprang up sheer to the distant roof. But Gagool gave us no time to stand and stare. On she hobbled, calling to us to follow. Straight to the end of the vast and silent cave she went, till we came to another doorway.

"Are you brave enough to enter the Place of Death?" she asked with a little cackle, and tap, tap, went her stick down the passage, as she trotted along, chuckling to herself.

We followed her. After about twenty paces I found myself in a gloomy cavern some forty feet long by thirty broad. At a first glance all I could make out was a huge stone table with a tall white figure at its head and smaller white figures all round it. Next I made out a brown thing seated on the table in the centre, and in another moment my eyes grew used to the light and I saw what all these things were.

I turned to run and would have been out of that place in a moment if Sir Henry had not caught me by the arm. Next second his eyes got used to the light, too, and he let go of me and began to mop the sweat off his forehead. As for Good he swore feebly, while Foulata threw her arms round his neck and shrieked.

Only Gagool chuckled loud and long.

It was a ghastly sight. At the end of the long stone table, holding in his bony fingers a great white spear, sat *Death* himself, in the shape of a great human skeleton, fifteen feet high. Up above his head he held the spear as though ready to strike; one bony hand rested on the table before him, and he was bent forward so that the skull was turned towards us, the jaws open a little, as though it were about to speak.

"Great heavens!" said I, faintly. "What can it be?"

"And what are those things?" said Good, pointing to the white

company round the table.

"And what is *that thing?*" asked Sir Henry, pointing to the brown creature seated on the table.

"Hee, hee, hee!" laughed Gagool. "To those who enter the Hall of the Dead, evil comes. Hee, hee, hee! Come, Incubu, come and see him you sent here," and the old hag caught Curtis' coat in her skinny fingers and led him towards the table. We followed.

Presently she stopped and pointed at the brown object on the table. Sir Henry looked and started back with a little cry; and no wonder, for there, seated, quite naked, on the table, its head resting on its knees, was the body of Twala. Over the surface of the corpse there was a thin, glassy film. I wondered what it could be and the next moment saw that, from the roof of the place, water was falling steadily, *drip! drop! drip!,* on to the neck of the corpse, from whence it ran down over the body. *Twala was being turned into a stalagmite.*

A look at the white forms seated on the stone bench that ran around that ghastly board showed that they were all stalagmites. This was the way in which the Kukuana people preserved their royal dead. They placed them for a long period of years under the drip, until they were iced over and preserved for ever by the silicious fluid.

I counted them. There were twenty-seven, the last being Ignosi's father. And the huge Death, sitting at the head of the board, had been hewn out of a single stalagmite.

Such was the White Death and such were the White Dead!

Chapter Nineteen
The Treasure Chamber

I had seen enough of this ghastly place.

"Gagool," I said in a low voice, "lead us to the chamber."

She leered up into my face. "My lords are not afraid?" she asked

"Lead on."

"Good, my lords," and she hobbled round to the back of th
great Death. "Here is the chamber. Let my lords light the lam
and enter."

She placed the gourd full of oil upon the floor and leaned he
self against the side of the cave. I took out a match, of which
still had a few in a box, and lit the rush wick. Then I looked f
the doorway. There was nothing before us but solid rock. Gago
grinned. "The way is there, my lords."

"Do not make fools of us," I said sternly.

"I jest not, my lords. See!" and she pointed at the rock.

I held up the lamp and saw that a mass of stone was slowl
rising from the floor and vanishing into the rock above. It mu
have moved upon some simple balance principle, but how
worked none of us saw. Gagool saw to that, but I have littl
doubt that there was some very simple lever that she had presse
Very slowly and gently the great stone raised itself till at last
dark hole showed itself, about ten feet high and five across,
the place which it had filled.

My excitement was so great that I began to tremble and shak
Would it prove a hoax? Or was old da Silvestra right? Were w

about to become the richest men in the world? We should know in a minute or two.

"Enter, white men from the stars," said Gagool, stepping into the doorway, "but first hear Gagool the old. The bright stones that you will see were dug out of the pit over which the Silent Ones are set, and stored here, I know not by whom, or why they left this place. But it happened, many years ago, that a white man reached this country from over the mountains, and was well received by the king of the day. He it is who sits yonder," and she pointed to the fifth king at the table of the dead. "And it came to pass that a woman of the country who had learned the secret of the door brought the white man to this place. He found the stones and filled a goatskin bag with them. And as he was going from the chamber he took up one more stone, a large one, and held it in his hand." Here she paused.

"Well," I asked, "what happened to da Silvestra?"

The old hag stared at mention of the name.

"How is it that you know the dead man's name?" she asked sharply; and then, without waiting for an answer, went on: "None know what happened; but it came about that the man was frightened, for he flung down the goatskin bag and fled with only one stone in his hand. *That* the king took, and it is the stone that you, Macumazahn, took from Twala's brows."

"Have none entered here since?" I asked.

"None, my lord. But you may do so. If I speak truth the goatskin with the stones will lie upon the floor."

She hobbled through the doorway, taking the light with her.

"Hang it all," said Good, "I'm not going to be frightened by that old devil." and followed by Foulata, who was shivering with fear, he plunged into the passage, and we quickly followed.

After some yards Foulata said that she felt faint and would wait there. We sat her on a stone block and left her to recover.

Fifteen paces farther on we came to a painted wooden door. It was standing wide open. *Across the threshold lay a goatskin bag that seemed to be full of pebbles.*

"What did I tell you?" sniggered Gagool.

Good stooped and lifted it. It was heavy and jingled.

"By Jove! I believe it's full of diamonds," he said in an awed whisper.

"Go on," said Sir Henry impatiently. "Here, old lady, give me the lamp," and taking it from Gagool's hand, he stepped through the doorway. We pressed in after him, forgetful for the moment of the bag of diamonds, and found ourselves in Solomon's treasure chamber.

The room had been cut out of the rock and was no more than ten feet square. Piled at one side, as high as the roof, was a fine collection of elephant tusks, enough ivory to make a man wealthy for life. But my eye was caught by something on the other side of the room—about a score of wooden boxes, something like ammunition boxes, only rather larger and painted red.

"There are the diamonds," I cried. "Bring the light."

Sir Henry did so. The lid of the top box had been smashed in, probably by da Silvestra himself. I put my hand through the hole and drew it out full, not of diamonds, but of gold pieces of a shape that none of us had seen before.

"Ah!" I said, replacing the coins, "we shan't go home empty-handed. There must be a couple of thousand pieces in each box, and there are eighteen boxes."

"The stones, the stones!" put in Gagool, pointing. "Let my lords look there, where it is darkest, if they would find the stones."

"Look in that corner, Curtis," I said, indicating the spot Gagool had pointed out. He went to it.

"There's a recess," he said. "Great heavens! Look here!"

We hurried to where he was standing in a kind of nook. Against the wall were placed three stone chests, each about two feet square. Two were fitted with stone lids; the lid of the third rested against the side of the chest, which was open.

"Look!" Curtis said, holding the light over the open chest. At first I could see nothing but a dazzling, silvery sheen. When my eyes got used to it I saw that the chest was three parts full of uncut diamonds, mostly large in size. Stooping, I picked some up. Yes, there was no mistake about it, there was the unmistakable soapy feeling about them.

I gasped as I dropped them. "We are the richest men in the world," I said.

"We shall flood the market with diamonds," said Good.

"Got to get them there first," suggested Sir Henry.

"Hee, hee, hee!" went old Gagool behind us. "There are the bright stones that you love, white men. Take them, run them through your fingers. *Eat* of them, hee, hee! *Drink* of them, ha, ha!"

I began to laugh at the idea of eating and drinking diamonds. I could not stop myself. And the others joined in, without knowing why. There we stood and shrieked with laughter over millions of pounds' worth of diamonds, just waiting to be taken away.

Suddenly the fit passed off and we stopped laughing.

"Open the other chests," croaked Gagool. "Take your fill, white lords."

We set to work to pull up the stone lids on the other two. They also were full to the brim. We feasted our eyes upon them.

Not one of us saw Gagool creep out of the treasure chamb
and down the passage. Then came a cry from Foulata:

"Oh, Bougwan! Help! Help!—the rock falls!"

"Leave go, girl! Then—"

"Help! Help! She has stabbed me!"

By then we were running down the passage. The light fro
the lamp showed the rock door slowly closing down. Near
struggled Foulata and Gagool. The girl's blood had run dow
to her knee. Gagool broke away from her and threw herself o
the ground to twist like a snake through the crack of the fallin
stone. She was under—ah, God! too late! The stone nipped h
and she yelled in agony. Down, down it came, all the thirty tor
of it, slowly pressing her old body against the rock below. Shrie
upon shriek, then a long, sickening *crunch*. The door was shu
just as we hurled ourselves against it.

Chapter Twenty

We Abandon Hope

We turned to Foulata. She had been stabbed in the body an
could not, I saw, live long.

"Ah! Bougwan, I die!" gasped the beautiful creature. "She crep
out—Gagool. I did not see her, I was faint—and the door be
gan to fall; then she came back and was looking up the path—
and I saw her and caught her and held her, and she stabbed me
and *I die*, Bougwan."

"Poor girl!" cried Good, and then, as he could do nothing else
he fell to kissing her.

"Is Macumazahn there?" she said, after a pause. "It grows so dark, I cannot see."

"Here I am, Foulata."

"Macumazahn, be my tongue for a moment—I would speak a word to Bougwan."

"Say on, Foulata."

"Say to my lord, Bougwan, that—I love him. Say that if I live again, perhaps I shall see him in the stars, and that—I will search them all for him. Say no more, save that I love—Oh, hold me close, Bougwan, I cannot feel your arms—*oh, oh!*"

"She's dead!" said Good, rising in grief, the tears running down his face.

"You need not let that trouble you, old fellow," said Sir Henry gently.

"Eh!" said Good. "What do you mean?"

"I mean that you will soon be in a position to join her. *Man, don't you see that we are buried alive?*"

Until he spoke I do not think the full horror of what had happened had come home to us. But now we understood. The great rock door had closed upon us and the only brain which knew its secret was crushed to powder beneath it. And we were on the wrong side of it!

We stood there horrified, beside the body of Foulata. We saw it all now: Gagool had planned this snare for us from the first. I saw, now, the point of that sneer about eating and drinking the diamonds.

"This will never do," said Sir Henry hoarsely; "the lamp will soon go out. Let us see if we can find the spring that works the rock."

We sprang forward and began to feel up and down the door

and the sides of the passage. But no knob or spring could we find.

"It doesn't work from the inside," I said at last. "If it did, Gagool would not have risked trying to crawl beneath."

"At all events," said Sir Henry, with a hard little laugh, "hers was almost as awful an end as ours is likely to be. We can do nothing with the door. Let's go back to the treasure room."

We turned and went and, as we did so, I saw by the wall the basket of food which poor Foulata had carried. I took it up and brought it back with me to the treasure chamber that was to be our grave. Then we went back and carried in Foulata's corpse, laying it on the floor by the boxes of coins.

Next we seated ourselves, leaning our backs against the three stone chests. Then we divided the food. It would, we thought, make four small meals for each of us. We had, besides, two gourds of water, each holding about a quart.

"Now," said Sir Henry, "let us eat and drink, for tomorrow we die."

We each ate a small piece of biltong and drank a sip of water. Then we sat in silence for some time. The lamp began to burn dim.

"Quatermain," said Sir Henry, "what is the time—your watch goes?"

It was six o'clock. We had entered the cave at eleven.

"Infadoos will miss us," I said. "If we do not return tonight, he will search for us in the morning."

"He'll search in vain," Curtis said. "He doesn't know the secret of the door, nor even where it is. The search for treasure has brought many to a bad end; we shall swell their number."

The lamp grew dimmer yet.

Presently it flared up and showed us the whole scene, the mass of white tusks, the boxes full of gold, the corpse of poor Foulata stretched before us, the goatskin full of treasure, the dim glimmer of the diamonds, and the wild, wan faces of my friends seated there awaiting death by starvation.

Suddenly the light sank, and went out.

Chapter Twenty-One
The Tunnel

Even now I shudder to recall the horrors of that night. I found it impossible to sleep much—the silence itself was too great to allow it. We were cut off from all the sounds and echoes of the world. We were as already dead.

I thought often of the treasures that lay around us and would gladly have bartered them all for the faintest chance of escape. Soon, no doubt, we should be glad to exchange them for a bit of food or a cup of water. Truly wealth, which men spend all their lives seeking, is a useless thing at the end.

And so the night wore on.

"Good," said Sir Henry's voice at last, and it sounded awful in the intense stillness, "how many matches have you in the box?"

"Eight, Curtis."

"Strike one and let us see the time."

He did so. In the dense darkness the flame nearly blinded us. It was five o'clock by my watch. Dawn would be breaking on the snowy peaks far over our heads.

"We had better eat something to keep up our strength," I said.

"What's the use of eating?" asked Good. "The sooner we die and get it over the better."

"While there's life there's hope," said Sir Henry.

We ate and sipped some water, and another period of time passed. Somehow the day went by, and when I lit a match to see the time it was seven o'clock.

Once more we ate and drank, and as we did so an idea came to me.

"How is it," I asked, "that the air in this place keeps fresh?"

"Great heavens!" said Good, starting up. "I never thought of that. It can't come through the stone door, for it is airtight, if ever a door was. It must come from somewhere. Let's have a look."

This spark of hope brought about a change in us. For more than an hour we groped about the place on our hands and knees, feeling for any sign of a draught. At last Sir Henry and I gave up in despair, but Good carried on searching. Presently he said, in an odd sort of voice: "I say, you fellows, come here."

In the gloom we scrambled towards him.

"Quatermain, put your hand here where mine is. Now, do you feel anything?"

"*I think* I feel air coming up."

"Listen." He stamped upon the place and a flame of hope shot up in our hearts. *It rang hollow.*

With trembling hands I lit a match, one of the last three. We were in the angle of the far corner of the chamber, which was why we had not seen the join in the solid rock floor, and, great heavens!—there, let in level with the rock, was a stone ring!

We said no word. Good took out his pocket knife and scratched away at the ring with it. Finally he got it under and levered

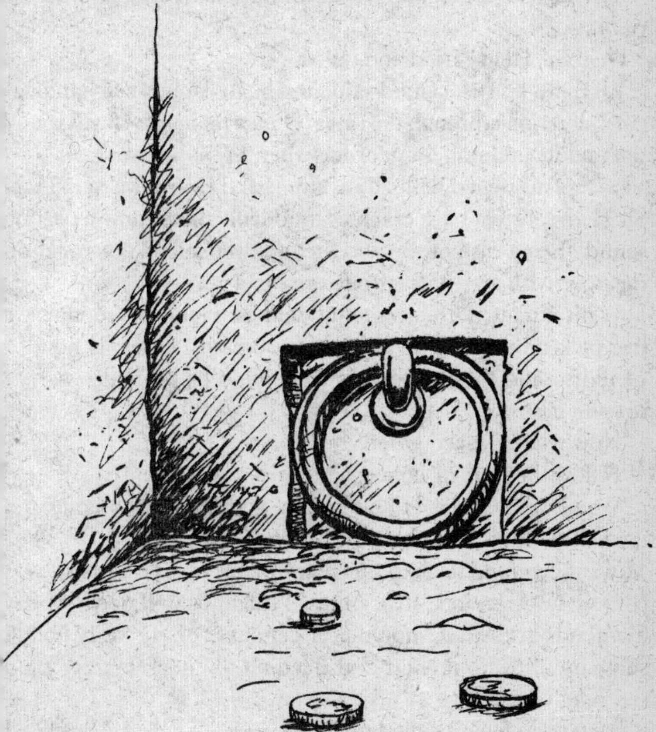

away gently for fear of breaking the hook. The ring began to move. Soon it was upright. He got his hands to it and tugged, but nothing moved.

"Let me try," I said. I took hold and strained away, but with no result.

Then Sir Henry tried and failed.

"All right, Curtis," Good said, and he took out a silk handkerchief and ran it through the ring. "Quatermain, get Curtis round the middle and pull for dear life when I give the word. *Now.*"

Each of us pulled with all his strength. I heard the muscles of Sir Henry's great back cracking. Suddenly there came a parting sound, then a rush of air, and then we were all on our backs on the floor with a great flagstone on top of us.

"Light a match, Quatermain," said Sir Henry, as soon as we had picked ourselves up and got our breath, "carefully now."

I did so and there before us was—God be praised!—*the first step of a stone stair.*

"Now what?" asked Good.

"Follow the stair, of course, and trust to Providence."

"Wait," said Curtis. "Quatermain, get the bit of biltong and the water that is left; we may need them."

I went creeping back to our place by the chests, and as I was coming away an idea struck me—I might as well pocket a few diamonds in case we should ever get out of this ghastly hole. I stuck my fist into a chest and filled all the pockets of my old shooting coat.

"Won't you fellows take some diamonds?" I called. "I've filled my pockets."

"Oh! Hang the diamonds!" said Curtis. "I hope that I never see another."

Good made no answer. He was, I think, taking a last farewell of the poor girl who had loved him.

"Come on," said Sir Henry, who was already standing on the first step of the stone stair. "Steady, I'll go first."

He started down, counting the steps as he went. When he got to "fifteen" he stopped.

"Here's the bottom," he said. "Thank goodness! I think it's a passage. Come on down."

Good went next and I followed. On reaching the bottom I lit one of the two remaining matches. By its light we could just see that we were standing in a narrow tunnel, which ran right and left at right angles to the staircase. Before we could make out any more the match burned my fingers and went out. Which way should we turn? One way might lead us to safety, the other to destruction. We had no idea, till suddenly it struck Good that when I had lit the match the draught of the passage blew the flame to the left.

"Let us go against the draught," he said: "air draws inwards, not outwards."

We set off, feeling our way along the wall and testing the ground before every step. When we had groped our way for about a quarter of an hour, the passage took a sharp turn, or was cut across by another, which we followed, only in course of time to be led into a third. It struck me that we must be in the ancient workings of a mine.

At last we halted, thoroughly worn out and somewhat sick at heart. Had we, I wondered, escaped Death in the darkness of the chamber only to meet him in the darkness of the tunnels?

We ate the last of our biltong and drank our last sup of water. As we stood there, I thought I caught a sound, to which I called

the attention of the others. It was very faint and very far off, but it *was* a sound, a faint murmuring sound.

"By heavens!" said Good. "It's running water—come on!"

Off we started again in the direction from which the murmur came. It grew louder all the time. On, yet on; now we could make out the unmistakable swirl of rushing water. Now we were quite near to it, and Good, who was leading, swore that he could smell it.

"Go gently, Good," Sir Henry warned. "We must be close."

Splash! and a cry from Good. He had fallen in.

We shouted to him. An answer came back in a choky voice, "All right; I've got hold of a rock. Strike a light to show me where you are."

I lit my last match. Its faint gleam showed a dark mass of water running at our feet. Some way out was the dark form of Good hanging on to a rock.

"Stand clear to catch me," he called. "I'll swim for it."

We heard a splash and a great struggle. Another minute and he had hold of Sir Henry's outstretched hand, and we had pulled him up high and dry into the tunnel.

"My word!" he said between gasps. "That was touch and go! It runs like a millrace, and I could feel no bottom."

It was clear that this would not do. After Good had rested a little, and we had drunk our fill from the water of the underground river, which was sweet and fresh, we turned back along the tunnel, Good dripping unpleasantly in front of us. At length we came to another tunnel leading to our right.

"We may as well take it," said Sir Henry wearily. "All roads are alike here."

Slowly, for a long, long while, we stumbled, utterly weary, along

this new tunnel, Sir Henry leading now. Suddenly he stopped and we bumped up against him.

"Look," he whispered, "is my brain going, or is that light?"

We stared with all our eyes. Yes, there far ahead of us was a faint, glimmering spot. With a sort of gasp of hope we pushed on. In five minutes there was no longer any doubt; it *was* a patch of faint light. A minute more and a breath of real fresh air was fanning us. On we struggled. All at once the tunnel narrowed. Sir Henry went on his knees. Smaller yet it became, till it was only the size of a fox's earth—it was earth now, mind you, the rock had ceased.

A squeeze, a struggle, and Sir Henry was out, and so was Good, and so was I, and there above us were the blessed stars and in our nostrils was the sweet air. Then suddenly something gave and we were all rolling over and over through grass and bushes and soft, wet soil.

I caught at something and stopped. I sat up and shouted. An answer came from just below, where Sir Henry was sitting on some level ground. I scrambled to him and found him unhurt, though breathless. Then we looked for Good. A little way off we found him too, jammed in a forked root.

We got him out and sat down together on the grass. Surely the Lord God himself must have guided our footsteps to the jackal hole at the end of the tunnel. We were out, and there on the mountains the dawn we had never thought to look upon again was blushing rosy red.

Presently the grey light stole down the slopes and we saw that we were nearly at the bottom of the vast pit in front of the entrance to the cave. Now we could make out the dim forms of the three stone idols who sat upon its edge. No doubt those awful

passages along which we had wandered through the night had been, in some way, connected with the great diamond mine.

Lighter it grew, and lighter yet. We could see each other now; gaunt, hollow-eyed wretches, smeared all over with dust and mud, bruised, bleeding and with the long fear of death still upon our faces.

We rose, and with slow and painful steps we struggled up the sloping side of the great pit. At last it was done and we stood on the road on the side opposite the statues.

By the side of the road, a hundred yards off, a fire was burning in front of some huts, and round the fire were figures. We made towards them. Presently one of the figures rose, saw us, and fell on the ground, crying out in fear.

"Infadoos!" I yelled. "Infadoos! It is us, your friends."

He ran to us, staring wildly, and still shaking with fear.

"Oh, my lords, my lords, it is indeed you come back from the dead!—come back from the dead!"

And the old warrior flung himself down before us and clasped Sir Henry's knees, and wept aloud for joy.

Chapter Twenty-Two
Found

For two days we rested, then set off back to Loo, where Ignosi listened with breathless interest to our wonderful story.

"The time has come for us to bid you farewell, Ignosi," I said. "Behold, you came with us a servant and now we leave you a mighty king."

He covered his face with his hands.

"Your words split my heart in two," he said at last. "Well, you must go and leave my heart sore. Infadoos, my uncle, shall guide you with an escort. There is, I have learned, another way across the mountains that he shall show you. Farewell, my brothers. Fare you well for ever, Incubu. Macumazahn, and Bougwan, my lords and my friends."

We went in silence.

Next day at dawn we left Loo with Infadoos and the regiment of Buffaloes. Early as the hour was, all the main street of the town was lined with crowds of people who gave us the royal salute as we passed.

Infadoos told us that there was a place in the mountains where it was possible to climb down the wall of cliff that separated Kukuanaland from the desert. It seemed that some years ago a party of Kukuana hunters had gone by this path into the desert in search of ostriches, whose plumes were much prized. In the course of their hunt they had been led far from the mountains, and were much troubled by thirst. Seeing trees on the horizon, they made towards them and found a large oasis, plentifully watered. It was by way of this oasis that Infadoos suggested we return, and the idea seemed to us a good one. Some of the ostrich-hunters were with our party to guide us to the oasis, from which, they said, they could see more fertile spots far away in the desert.

In the evening of the fourth day's journey we found ourselves once more on the crest of the mountains, about twenty-five miles to the north of Sheba's Breasts. At dawn next day we were led to a cliff down which ran a track that would take us down to the desert two thousand feet below.

We said goodbye to that true friend, Infadoos, who wished a[
good upon us and nearly wept with grief. We were very sorry t[
part from him. Then, with five guides carrying food and wate[
we began our ladder-like descent. It was a long and difficu[
business, but somehow that evening we found ourselves at th[
bottom.

"Do you know," said Sir Henry that night, as we sat by ou[
fire, "I think that there are worse places than Kukuanaland i[
the world."

"I almost wish I were back," said Good with a sigh.

For myself, I was glad that my old shooting coat still held enoug[
treasure to make us all wealthy men. We had not done so bad[
after all.

Next morning we started our march across the desert, and b[
midday of the third day's journey we could see the trees of th[
oasis. An hour before sundown we were once more walking upo[
grass and hearing the sound of running water.

I was walking some way in front of the other two, along th[
bank of a stream, when suddenly I stopped and rubbed my eye[
There, not twenty yards ahead, under the shade of a fig tre[
was a cosy hut with a full-length door.

"What the dickens," I said to myself, "can a hut be doing here[
Even as I said it, the door opened and there limped out of it[
white man clothed in skins and with a huge black beard. I thoug[
that I must have got a touch of the sun. It was impossible. N[
hunter ever came to such a place as this. I stared and stare[
and so did the other man. Sir Henry and Good came up.

"Look there," I said. "Is that a white man, or am I mad?"

Sir Henry stared, and Good stared. Then all of a sudden th[
lame white man gave a great cry and came hobbling towar[

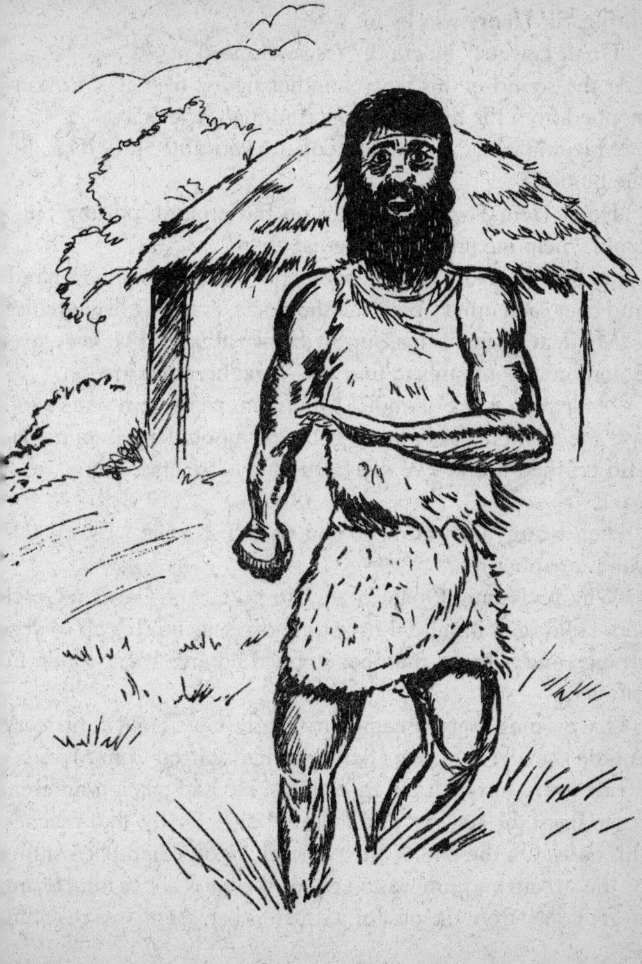

us. When he got close he fell down in a sort of faint. With a spring, Sir Henry was by his side.

"Great Powers!" he cried. "*It's my brother George!*"

At the sound of his voice another figure, also clad in skins, stepped from the hut and came running towards us.

"Macumazahn," he called, "you not know me? Jim, Baas, Jim the hunter!"

"Here, Henry," said the man on the ground, putting out a hand, "help me up, there's a good chap."

Sir Henry did so, and they pumped away at each other's hands and beat each other about the shoulders, laughing like lunatics.

"My dear chap," burst out Sir Henry at last. "I've been over Solomon's Mountains to find you—and here you are!"

"I *tried* to go over Solomon's Mountains nearly two years ago," was the answer, "but when I got here, a boulder fell on my leg and crushed it and I've not been able to go either forward or back."

Then I came up. "How do you do, Mr. Neville," I said. "Do you remember me?"

"Why, it's Hunter Quatermain," he said. "And Captain Good, too. Hold on a minute. I'm getting dizzy again. It's all so very strange and, when a man has stopped hoping, it's a wonderful moment."

That evening over the camp fire George Curtis told us his story. A little short of two years before he had started from Sitanda's Kraal to try to reach the mountains. He had taken a different route from the one we had followed and, finally, had reached this oasis. On the day of their arrival, George had been sitting by the stream and Jim was on top of the bank above him, trying to get honey from the nest of a stingless bee. As he was reaching

out, he loosened a boulder which fell upon George Curtis's right leg and crushed it. He was made so dreadfully lame that he found it impossible to go forward or back. However, they had got on pretty well for food by shooting or trapping the game which came to the oasis at night.

After hearing all this, Sir Henry told him of our adventures, sitting late into the night to do it.

"By Jove!" George said, when I showed him some of the diamonds, "well, at least you have something for your pains, besides my worthless self!"

This remark set me thinking and, having spoken to Good, I told Sir Henry that it was our wish that he should take a third share of the diamonds, or if he would not, that his share should be given to his brother, who had suffered even more than ourselves in his attempt to find them. We got Sir Henry to agree that his brother should take his share, but George Curtis did not know of it till some time afterwards.

*   *   *   *   *   *   *

And at this point I think I shall end this history. Our journey back across the desert to Sitanda's Kraal was difficult, as we had to support George Curtis, but we managed it in the end. Weeks later we were all safe and sound at my little place near Durban, where I am now writing, and from which I now say farewell to all those who have come with me throughout the strangest trip I ever made in the course of my life.

Allan Quatermain

Illustrated Chosen Classics ────── *Retold* ──────

Titles available in this series: